THIS IS SHYNESS

THIS IS

Leanne Hall lives in Melbourne and works as a children's specialist at an independent bookstore. Leanne can't think of anything better than a life spent reading and writing young adult fiction, and has far too many future books living in her head to ever consider a full-time job. *This Is Shyness* is her first novel.

LEANNE HALL

SHYNESS

WITHDRAWN

TEXT PUBLISHING MELBOURNE AUSTRALIA

The paper used in this book is manufactured only from wood grown in sustainable regrowth forests.

The Text Publishing Company
Swann House
22 William Street
Melbourne Victoria 3000
Australia
textpublishing.com.au

First published in 2010 by The Text Publishing Company

Cover design by W.H. Chong
Text design by Susan Miller
Typeset by J&M Typesetting
Printed and bound by Griffin Press

National Library of Australia
Cataloguing-in-Publication entry

Hall, Leanne Michelle, 1977-

This is shyness / Leanne Hall.

1st ed.

ISBN: 9781921656521 (pbk.)

For young adults.

A823.4

For Mum and Dad

1

The bouncer stares at my ID, his expression murky, his face tinted purple by the neon sign above us. I rub my bare arms. The temperature must have dropped five degrees in the last few minutes.

Neil hovers behind us, just inside the swing doors. He's still wearing his work shirt, and everything about him is limp and sweaty. He twitches as if he's about to step in and say something. I widen my eyes, trying to send him a telepathic message. *Leave it to me. I have this under control.*

The bouncer looks down from his concrete stoop with bloodhound eyes. He's worked too many nights in a row. I push my shoulders back in my too-tight t-shirt. This is up to me and the motivational powers of my two best assets. The bouncer knows my mum's old driver's licence is a joke. I know he knows it's a joke. He knows I know he knows. He's just trying to do his job.

'What's your star sign?' he says eventually. Predictable.

'Leo. What's yours?'

That gets a tired smile out of him. He's not such a tough guy. His puffa jacket gives him bulk that he doesn't have.

'Don't believe in that stuff, do I?'

'You look cold. You want me to bring you out a coffee?'

'No, thanks. You go inside and have a good night'—he runs his eyes over the licence one more time before handing it to me with a knowing smile—'*Maree*.'

Neil ushers me into the warmth of the pub. The doors thump behind us and I let my breath whoosh out with relief.

'Welcome to the Diabetic Hotel, l'il lady.'

Neil's hand rests a second too long on the small of my back. I'm so happy to get through the door I decide to let him get away with the patronising names just this once.

'So, you'll be going straight to the bar then?'

Neil salutes and swerves off to find us a drink. I flex my hands. There are crescent-shaped marks on my palms where I've dug my nails in.

I push past a cigarette machine and through another

set of swing doors to the main bar. The pub is smaller inside than I expected, but busy. The room is lit with sickly fluorescents that make everyone look jaundiced. I'm glad to see Rosie has already found a free table in a corner. I make my way over, and squeeze onto a tall stool.

Rosie grips my arm. 'I'm so glad you got in. I thought you were a goner.'

'I had it under control,' I say, and then ruin the effect by trying to sling my handbag onto the table and missing by a mile. I bend down to pick it up, trying not to touch the seriously manky carpet. The room wobbles as I straighten up, and I almost slip off the stool. This seat is designed for people at least a foot taller than me. We drank two bottles of wine between the three of us at Neil's house. I don't normally drink. I should slow down or I'll make a fool of myself. I don't want Neil and Rosie to think I can't hold my booze.

'This isn't what I was expecting.' Rosie takes in the room dubiously. I can tell by what she's wearing that she was expecting Neil to take us somewhere ritzier. Her halter dress gapes dangerously.

'Rosie…' I point at her chest.

'Whoops!' She makes a shocked face and pulls her dress up higher. 'Thanks, mate.'

'You nearly gave everyone a free look.'

'You can talk! Did your t-shirt shrink in the wash?'

3

It's a fair point. I bought this top to annoy my mum, but instead of telling me off, she asked if she could borrow it. Raving nympho is a popular look in our household.

'Ladies!' Neil puts a jug of beer and glasses on the table. He's making some sort of weird stud-face at us. 'What do you think of the Diabetic?'

What do I think? The pub is full of grandpas, suits and meat-heads. The walls are puke-green and decorated with ancient sports plaques. I don't want to go near the sticky table, and the vinyl seat on my stool is ripped. There's a U-shaped counter, a pool table and a beat-up jukebox. I don't mind rough, I'm used to rough, but Neil looks so pleased with himself you'd think he'd flown us to Paris for the evening.

'It's very…atmospheric.' Rosie takes a slug of beer and smiles at Neil blearily. I think she likes him. It's probably the only time in the history of the universe that someone has fancied Neil. Maybe I should leave them to it.

I take a sip of beer and it fizzes unpleasantly on my lips. I don't even like beer. I put my glass back on the table. Five minutes before I pick up my drink again, that's a promise. I squint at the clock behind the bar but the hands are frozen on the wrong time. It must be at least ten. I have a test on Monday that I should be studying for all weekend, but tonight I'm on a mission to forget. I normally say no to Neil's invitations but I don't want to sit at home alone. I don't want

4

to hear Mum coming in late with her internet date in tow, giggling and drunk. I don't want to eat breakfast while some geek saunters around our kitchen in his socks like he owns it.

I let my attention wander while Neil whispers something in Rosie's ear and she laughs loudly. I don't know how she can stand having him sit so close to her. Neil keeps 'accidentally' brushing his arm against mine, so I guess he's still hedging his bets. I move away, wrapping my arms around my handbag and resting my chin on it.

The room is subdued. The only rowdy group is the suits playing a drinking game at the next table. Their table is littered with shot glasses. One of them catches me staring and winks. Pervert. I'm young enough to be his daughter. I look away.

And then I see him.

Sitting on the far side of the counter where the light doesn't quite reach, on his own. A young guy, not much older than me, with pale skin and dark hair crawling everywhere. He plays with something small and silver on the counter, turning it over in his hands. The hair on his forearms is thick below his rolled-up shirtsleeves. Heavy forehead, full lips. He shouldn't be able to get away with his ridiculous urban cowboy quiff, but he does.

I turn back to Neil and Rosie. The last thing a boy that good-looking needs is one more girl checking him out.

5

Rosie and Neil are both laughing and looking like they expect me to get the joke too, so I smile. Rosie has lipstick on her front teeth. I sip my beer again and resolve to concentrate on the conversation. They're saying something about the receptionist at work. I hate talking about work.

But then I can't help myself: I *have* to look at him again.

He's finishing his drink, tipping his head back to drain the glass. Then his gaze roams the room like he's expecting someone. I hold my breath and bite my lip.

He sees me.

His eyes connect with mine and I get this tingly feeling that travels all the way from my stomach to my fingers and toes. I stare back. One second, two seconds, three. I probably couldn't look away even if I wanted to.

Eventually he blinks and breaks the thread between us. I feel a jolt of disappointment. He stands up and slips his wallet into his jeans pocket.

'Oy!' Neil zooms in so close I can smell his beer breath. He squeezes my arm. 'Rosie says you're the most ticklish person she's ever met. Is that true?'

I push Neil's hand away and lean around him, trying to see what the guy is doing. Is he leaving? Why would he leave after looking at me like that?

The beautiful boy ambles in the direction of our table,

his head lowered. He's much taller than I expected and he looks great in tight black jeans and a checked vintage shirt. I sit up and flick my hair off my shoulders.

Neil pokes his finger right into my gut, hard and without warning.

'Stop it!' I growl, slapping at him wildly. I hate people touching my stomach. One of my hands connects with the side of Neil's head but it doesn't stop him. He lunges for me and I double over, trying to protect myself. I feel the stool lift and tilt sideways in slow motion. I grab for the edge of the table, but it's too late—I'm falling.

two

I'm most of the way across the room before I realise I have no idea what I'm going to say to her. She lies on the floor of the pub, her hair fanned out in a black halo. The guy with the shaved head lies next to her. He might throw up, he's laughing so hard. The girl raises herself on her elbows, a murderous expression on her face.

My falling shadow looks ominous, even to me. She stares straight at me, with eyes rimmed heavily in eyeliner. She looks a hundred times better up close.

I blink. Why did I come over here in the first place?

In my panic I forget myself and do what I do best: I howl.

Every shred of longing and despair in the front bar—and believe me, on a Friday night at the Diabetic there's plenty of it—gets sucked into my lungs. My body shakes as the sound runs through me. The pub stereo shudders to a halt. Every face in the room turns towards me.

I finish with a couple of short sharp yelps and then I'm quiet.

Someone from the City snorts nervously. The regulars turn back to watch the football on the telly mounted above the bar. It's not as if this is the first time this has happened.

'You're a tool,' the girl says, in a cold voice that could cut through my ribs to my heart. The diamond stud in the curve of her nose flashes.

I came to the pub tonight because the walls were closing in on me at home. I thought I'd run into Paul or Thom here. Howling at hot strangers wasn't on my schedule.

'It's in my nature,' I reply, and incredibly she laughs. She brushes the guy's arm off like it's little more than a piece of lint.

'I was talking to Neil, not you,' she says. 'Are you going to help me up?'

Oh. I offer her a hand, and hoist her to her feet. She's light as anything.

'Can I buy you a drink?'

She hesitates and glances at her friends. The chubby

redhead in the evening dress stares. The guy—Neil—gets to his feet, with his hands clenched by his sides, his jaw clenched too. I raise both hands and back away. I've read this all wrong.

'I'll leave you alone. Enjoy your night.'

'Sure.' She twists her hair into a rope. 'You can buy me a drink.'

I swallow my surprise and walk her to my usual spot at the counter. I sense the old-timers watching us, regarding the girl appreciatively. I hold two fingers up to Robbie, the guy behind the bar. He bangs his hand against the stereo to restart it, and pours us two beers. He waves away my money. Pity beers. Or good luck beers. Either way, I'll need them.

'I'm Wolfboy.'

She shakes my hand. 'I guess that's something to do with the howling, right?'

'Right.' I put my glass on the counter, but then I don't know what to do with my hands. She's making me jumpy. I don't think I've ever seen skin so smooth and tanned before. Her eyelids are smeared with green glitter.

'So do you howl for all the ladies?'

I duck my head. What am I supposed to say to that?

'Hey, I'm just kidding around.' She touches my arm. 'I've never heard anything like it. How do you do it?'

'I don't know.'

'For a second I thought I'd hit my head *really* hard and was hearing things.'

'You haven't told me your name yet.'

She looks down at her t-shirt and then up at me. 'My name's Wildgirl; that's pretty obvious, isn't it?'

I don't trust myself to look where she's looking but I drop my eyes just long enough to see the word 'WILD-GIRL' plastered across the front of her chest.

'Yeah, but what's your real name?'

'Well, *Wolfboy*, what's your real name?'

'Everyone calls me Wolfboy. You can ask any of the Locals here.'

'So, I'll call you that, and you call me Wildgirl. Simple.'

I don't know if she means to, but her knees keep banging into mine every time she shifts on her barstool. She's wearing short shorts and white tights, and anyone who thinks brown eyes are boring needs to have their head read. Her skin is so peachy there's no way she's a Local.

I'm not sure if I'm looking at her too much or too little. My knuckles are white around my beer glass. I've never been much of a talker, but when I feel the space between us, her on her stool, me on mine, I want to fill it.

'Where are you from, Wildgirl?' She beams when I call her that.

'Plexus.'

I know it. Other side of the river.

11

I went to Plexus once while I was still at high school. I remember there was a closed-down amusement park on the beachfront. Thom and Paul and I threw rocks through the barred gate, trying to hit a clown statue, before we got bored and caught the train home again. That was a long time ago.

'What about your friends?' I nod in their direction. Wildgirl turns and waves at them.

'I work with them. Neil lives near here; that's why I'm on this side of town. I'm not sure about Rosie.'

Neil fires me a death stare over the top of his glass, while Rosie tries to distract him with chatter and cigarettes. I don't want to get into a fight, but there's no way I'm going to give up my seat next to Wildgirl to keep that guy happy. 'Looks like Neil's a fan of yours.'

'He's old enough—for it to be creepy.' Wildgirl drinks deeply. 'He's my supervisor at work. I don't normally hang out with him.'

'You're not a tourist to the dark side then?'

Her nose crinkles. It's so cute I want to think of as many ways as I can to give her that puzzled look.

'What do you mean?'

'You know that this pub's in Shyness, right?'

'Yeah. Neil said it's the suburb next to where he lives.'

'Did Neil also tell you that the sun doesn't rise here?'

She laughs loudly and unselfconsciously. She really has

no idea. Sometimes I forget that most outsiders don't care about what happens here. Her laughter falls away. 'You're serious, aren't you?'

I nod.

'Never rises? As in, never ever?'

'You can't tell now, not when it's night everywhere. But during the day when you cross Grey Street the Darkness closes over you.'

'Like someone dimming the lights?'

'All over Shyness. Total darkness.'

She rests her head on her hand. You can see her struggling to believe me. Trying to decide if I'm crazy or not. One of her fingers curls into a lock of hair, and a wristful of bangles slips down to her elbow. I'm not sure how much longer I can sit here without touching her.

'What about the moon? You must get some light from the moon.'

'The moon never lets me be.' I'm about to say more, but then I stop. I won't bore her with the details of my life.

She finishes her beer in one hit and slams the glass down.

'Let's go.' Wildgirl slips off her stool and hoicks her enormous red bag onto one shoulder.

'What?'

'You heard me. I'm sick of the pub, so let's go.'

'Where?'

'Take me to where the night starts. Take me to Grey Street.'

'You won't be able to see anything at the moment though. It's night-time all over the city.'

She shrugs. She may barely reach my shoulders but you can tell she'd dish it out in an argument. I glance around the room. Still no sign of Paul or Thom.

'Were you waiting for someone?'

'Just the guys in my band.' I can see Paul and Thom any night of the week. 'They weren't gonna be here for sure.' I stand and finish my beer. Robbie gives me a nod. Wildgirl and I walk across the room and towards the doors. I don't glance back but I know her friends are watching us every step of the way.

three

Wildgirl stands in the middle of Grey Street with her arms stretched out as if she's a religious leader. She pushes her fingers against the air, trying to prise it open. A siren rises and falls in the distance like a long, drawn-out whistle of appreciation.

I call out to her, 'You won't find anything. There's nothing there.' I hold her fire-engine handbag low by my side.

Behind Wildgirl the west side of the street operates normally. Late-night pizza shops spruik their wares with flashing lights. People lug shopping bags along the footpath without watching their backs. An ordinary shopping strip, crammed with hopeful immigrant businesses: Asian grocers, kebab shops, old-fashioned barbers, a shop selling belly-dancing costumes.

Grey Street is really two half-streets stitched together, with tram tracks running down the centre like a scar. The border between two worlds. It's been a while since I've been up this way. I've been bouncing between my house and the Diabetic for what feels like forever. Thom and Paul come over to rehearse and then we all go for a beer. When I need to eat, I find something. That's about as complicated as it gets.

The east side of Grey Street is a mess. The shops that aren't boarded up have broken windows and their insides are littered with drink cans, cigarette butts and broken glass. Graffiti splatters over every available surface. The smell of piss, fires and uncollected garbage hangs in the air. When you look up at night, the sky looks the same as in the west, but every streetlight is broken.

Wildgirl calls out, 'When did this happen?'

Locals pass by, eyeing the girl yelling in the middle of the road. People in Shyness don't normally stand around on the street having high-volume conversations. I sigh, and walk to the middle of the road so we don't have to yell at each other.

'It's been three years now. Something like that. It might have been a while before anyone noticed. First thing was the sun stopped rising all the way. At noon it sank back down in the east. It rose less and less each day until eventually it didn't show up at all.'

'And the other side is okay?'

'Grey Street's the border. This side: Shyness. The other side: Panwood.'

'What caused it?'

'I don't know. No one does.'

Wildgirl chews on this a while before speaking again. I shift her handbag from one arm to the other. It's heavier than it looks.

'Do you know anything about Greek gods?' she asks.

'Not much.'

'The Greek gods are just like mortals, always drunk and angry and getting it on with each other. The sun's supposed to be Apollo, the sun god, driving his fiery chariot across the sky every day.'

Wildgirl keeps talking as she crosses back to the foot-path without checking the road. She's lucky cars don't drive down here anymore. If I don't answer, maybe she'll stop chatting and we can get moving.

'So maybe Apollo got sick of driving his chariot?' she says. 'Maybe he's striking for better pay?'

I hand her bag back. She tucks it under her arm, still chasing her train of thought.

'Maybe he's gone on the dole and smokes bucket bongs all day?'

I'd smile but out of the corner of my eye I can see balls of shadow flitting up power poles, clustering on the powerlines like grapes. They're out tonight, lots of them. I walk faster, hoping Wildgirl will match my pace. Her bracelets jangle with each step.

'Everyone's got their theories,' I say. It drives me crazy listening to people crap on about the Darkness. I don't bother thinking about reasons; I just deal with it. If you don't like the night, leave.

I steer Wildgirl towards the Avenue. Maybe we can stop at Lupe's for a kebab before I stick her in a cab and send her home. I think Wildgirl would like Lupe. They've both got a crazy goddess vibe.

'There's only one way I'll believe you.' Wildgirl turns to face me. Her cheeks are flushed. 'We'll stay out all night. You show me around and I'll see for myself if the sun comes up in the morning.'

'It's not a good idea.' Even as I say the words part of me is thinking it's a great idea. It's been a long time since anyone has thought my life was interesting. I could make it seem that way, for a few hours.

'Why not?' She reaches into her handbag without breaking her stride and pulls out her phone. 'There. My phone's off. Mum can't call me. Not that she'll care what time I come home tonight.'

'You live with your mum?'

A pained look flashes across Wildgirl's face before she juts her chin out. 'Yeah, so what?'

I wonder where someone would learn so much about Greek mythology. I take a stab in the dark. 'What school do you go to?'

'What makes you think I'm still at school?'

'I can tell. You've got that jailbait thing going on.'

I can be mouthy too, when I want. I've had plenty of practice at the Diabetic, trying to get some respect from the regulars. It's difficult when some of the old guys remember me drinking raspberry lemonade in there with my dad.

'That's bullshit. I was at the pub with *work* friends, get it?'

'Didn't we already discuss that Neil wants to be more than just friends?'

I can tell she likes that, despite her irritation.

'Southside,' she admits eventually. 'Southside Girls' College.'

I don't know it. High school is a distant nightmare. I dropped out straight after my parents ran away to the country.

'So that makes you, what? Seventeen?'

'Yeah...and how old are you?'

'Eighteen. Almost nineteen.'

In nine months.

'Ooooh,' she cooes. 'So ancient, aren't you? So mature.'

'Look, I don't want to be responsible for an...outsider, not around here.' We come to a halt. Wildgirl faces me, her hands on her hips. Her hair almost crackles with electricity.

It's frustrating. Any guy would leap at the chance to spend time with a girl like this. But Shyness isn't a normal place and I'm not the most normal guy. I stare at Wildgirl's right shoulder instead of her face, to make this easier. It would be better for both of us if I walked her over to the far side of Panwood and put her in a cab. It would be better if I didn't think about holding her hand, showing her my favourite spots in Shyness, and talking until we can barely keep our eyes open.

'I can take care of myself. Mum and I live in a government flat, for godsake; I'm used to taking care of myself. I don't need you to protect me.'

I'd believe her too, if she knew what she was protecting herself from. I have that prickly feeling tonight that comes before trouble. It's been too quiet recently. No fights, no raids, no kidnappings. I risk a look at Wildgirl. Her eyes are huge and brimming with crocodile tears and hope. Like a Kidd. She's not that far past it.

I open my mouth to say something else in protest, anything, but Wildgirl beats me to it. She folds over as if someone has punched her.

'I have to go,' she says.

4

I need to pee.

One second I'm sparring with Wolfboy, and quite enjoying it to be honest, the next I feel as if my kidneys are going to explode. I don't even bother trying to hide my pain. I shouldn't have had the extra beer, but I wanted an excuse to talk to Wolfboy. Poor bladder control—there's a way to impress a man.

'I need to find somewhere to go.'

Wolfboy finally figures out what I mean. The crossed legs might have given it away.

'What are you, six years old? You should have gone at the pub.'

I attempt to hobble along the footpath and justify my

bodily functions at the same time. 'I didn't need to go when I was at the pub; otherwise, I would have, wouldn't I?'

Wolfboy sighs and throws his hands up. 'Let's cross the street and find somewhere.' He scours the nice side of Grey Street for options.

I calculate I have about thirty seconds left before I disgrace myself. There's no time to go begging in every shop. Squatting in an alley is beginning to look good when I spot a small functional building on the next corner. I stumble towards it. 'Look, there's a loo right here.'

The toilet is one of those automated ones, next to a nuclear-power-plant-bright convenience store. For some reason the store is covered in a large metal cage, as if it has a big-time orthodontic problem.

'You can't go in there.' Wolfboy sounds horrified. I'd like to see him stop me. I hobble towards the door.

'No way. Druggies have probably been using it.' Wolfboy grabs my arm and steers me away from the toilet, which, I must admit, looks like it's been designed for cyborgs. 'I know a bar near here where you can use the bathroom.'

'How far away?'

'Other side of the road. A minute's walk, at the most.'

Somehow I manage to keep up with Wolfboy, even though I can't actually stand up straight. We cross Grey Street and take a narrow one-way street into Panwood. True to Wolfboy's word it's not long before we stop at a nondescript doorway, the only interruption in an immense brick wall. I look through the door and into the stairwell.

'You didn't mention stairs. Stairs could push me over the edge.'

Wolfboy just rolls his eyes and takes me by the elbow again, dragging me upwards.

'It's all your fault.' If I keep talking I might stop thinking about how badly I need to go. 'If you hadn't plied me with beer we wouldn't be having this problem. Anyone would think that you were trying to make the poor, defenceless, under-age outsider drunk.'

The staircase ends abruptly in a darkened vestibule, and so does my rant. Every noise has been sucked from the air and replaced with a tasteful hush. A man in black appears from nowhere, ninja-style, to open the door for us. On the other side, another waiter greets us and leads us into the room.

The bar is super-ritzy: huge windows arching across two sides of the room, black chandeliers, leather benches, a perspex bar lit up like the mother ship. I'm stunned into silence. There's nothing in Plexus that comes close to this. The waiter gestures minimally for us to follow him. I feel like a participant in someone else's performance art.

Every woman in the place turns and stares at Wolfboy as we walk through the bar, skimming over me without interest. My cheeks are hot; I drop my head so my hair curtains my face. Wolfboy puts his hand on my back as we walk, but it's more like the touch of someone helping a little kid across the road than anything else.

Wolfboy sits in one of two armchairs next to an arched window and a low glass coffee table. The waiter pauses for a few agonising seconds while I refuse to sit, before handing me some menus and backing away.

Wolfboy points across the room as soon as the waiter is gone. 'Go towards where we came in, but turn left before you get there. You'll see a corridor.'

I chuck the menus on the table. To get to the bathroom I have to cross an expanse of carpet wide enough to give every single person in the room an opportunity to size me up, now that I'm not eclipsed by Wolfboy. All the women in here are rake-thin, devastatingly sophisticated and everyone—*everyone*—is dressed in black.

I walk as tall as I can, tugging my t-shirt down so it covers my marshmallow tummy. The carpet is so thick I feel like I'm walking in quicksand.

Thankfully the bathroom is easy to find. The first room is lined with Hollywood mirrors, the sort with lights around the edge, each with a separate vanity table and stool. Everything is raspberry and gold and glowing. A woman sits at one of the mirrors, fixing her hair. I rush through to the adjoining toilets and into the closest cubicle.

I pee for longer than I think is humanly possible, and then some. My brain had almost shut down under the strain of holding on. I flush and then sit on the closed toilet lid, taking a moment to gather my thoughts. My head rests on the cool wall next to me. The room spins gently when I close my eyes.

I imagine crossing Grey Street in the daytime. Would night fall over me gently like a velvety curtain? Or would the day turn dark in the blink of my eye? I don't really need to see the sunrise to know that Shyness is different. It's like there's a thin layer of static over everything that stops me from seeing what's really going on. People here scuttle around like they're scared of their own shadows. Even Wolfboy seems nervous. Maybe he's worried his girl-friend will bust him hanging out with another girl. Maybe he's already sick of my company and is trying to think of a polite way to ditch me.

When I wake up tomorrow there'll be only two days before I have to go back to school, with everyone staring and talking and laughing. Just like it was today. I don't know what's worse: the pitying looks or the disgusted ones.

I push those thoughts away. I'm here to have fun, not wallow.

The powder room is empty now, so I don't feel shy about laying my cheek against the flocked wallpaper. A chandelier sends shards of light around the room. I sit on a frighteningly fragile stool at one of the marble vanity tables and gaze at my reflection.

What am I doing, leaving the pub with a complete stranger, the strangest stranger I've ever met? I've got no idea whether the air of danger around Wolfboy is just part of a fashion statement or the real thing.

I smile to myself.

He's so hot.

If the girls at school could see me at this fancy bar with a guy this hot they'd be throwing up with jealousy.

It's a pity I look like I've been dragged backwards through a hedge. I didn't bring my handbag to the bathroom so I can't even touch up my make-up. I settle for smoothing down my hair and wiping the smudged eyeliner from under my eyes.

I need to turn myself back into Wildgirl who's not scared of anything. Wildgirl with no past.

Something glints on the very end vanity table. I scoot over for a closer look. It's a gold credit card, sitting all on its lonesome. Have people been snorting cocaine in here? I wipe my finger over the marble. It's clean.

The bankcard is slightly smaller than usual. *Future-Bank* must be a Shyness company because I've never heard of it. There's no name on the card, and no signature on the white strip on the back. It can't belong to the woman who was in here earlier because she was sitting at the table closest to the door. I look around and then feel stupid. The only people watching me are a dozen mirrored versions of myself. I slide the card into the back pocket of my shorts.

The trees outside scrape their twiggy fingers on the glass as if they want to be let in. I look out the window, beyond the reflected room and into the darkness. We float above the buildings around us, sailing on an ocean of black ink. On the very edge of the ocean there's a family of taller buildings that remind me of Plexus Commons. The buildings are freckled with lit-up windows; a full buttery moon rests above them.

I tear my eyes away from the night. The room looks like a carefully constructed bar scene in a movie—too slick and perfect to be real. I'm the youngest person here. Even if I were legal I'd still be the youngest by a mile.

I dissolve into the chair, hoping it will hide me in its winged arms. I want to tell Wolfboy about the mysterious card, but I don't want anyone to overhear and make me hand it in. You'd have to be pretty stupid or pretty drunk to leave your credit card lying around like that. People are still looking at us, probably wondering why Wolfboy would hang out with someone like me when clearly he could have his pick of the women here. The strange thing is that even the men are admiring him. Hot as he is, even I can see that Wolfboy's shirt is almost frayed through in places, and he looks like he hasn't been eating or sleeping or doing anything properly for a while now. The way everyone looks at him you'd think they want to be sleepless and hungry too.

'What is this place?'

'The Raven's Wing.' Wolfboy is strangely at ease in his brocade armchair and the opulent surroundings. His face is so sweet, but the rest of him, the hair and the muscles, belong to someone older. 'Bit over the top, isn't it?'

'I thought you were going to show me Shyness.'

'This will help you understand things.'

I don't see how sitting around with a bunch of people with clever haircuts will help me. They've probably never had to struggle for anything; they're the kind of people who don't know what it's like to really want something and not be able to have it. The kind of people Mum works for, cleaning their houses and doing their laundry. I'm the first to admit my mum is slightly ridiculous—her clothes are too tight, her make-up too thick—but you should see the way her clients speak to her sometimes.

'I want to leave. I don't like it here.'

The waiter stops and places two drinks theatrically on our table.

'We didn't order—' I start telling him.

'Thanks,' says Wolfboy, turning in his seat. A silver-haired man with square black-rimmed glasses waves at us from the bar. Wolfboy nods at him. 'Please. We'll have one drink here and then we'll return to Shyness. Trust me.'

I don't want to know if he can be trusted. It's not possible to trust anyone in this world. We're all here to take care of ourselves, and ourselves only. This is how I look at it: if a gunman rampaged through the flats, I'd barricade Mum and me in our place and forget about anyone else on our floor. If the gunman broke into our flat then I'm not entirely sure I'd take a bullet for Mum, or vice versa. When it comes down to it, we're all on our own. Once you realise that, life becomes simpler.

'How come everyone knows you? Is your band famous?'

'Maybe.'

Wolfboy doesn't say anything else. Every other musician I've ever met was dying to tell me about their band. When Wolfboy first mentioned it I was disappointed. Everyone my age wants to be singers or models or actors. Imagine a world where people idolised nurses or scientists or environmentalists. But at least he hasn't been crapping on about it. Maybe he's into music for the right reasons.

'What are you called?'

'The Long Blinks.'

I haven't heard of them, but I'm not surprised. My taste

in music is kind of unusual. I prefer the older, classier stuff. I don't watch reality TV and I have no idea what sort of shoes are in this week, so as you can imagine I have plenty to talk about with the other girls at school.

'Why are you called that?'

'The long blinks happen right before you go to sleep, when your mind fights it and your lids are heavy. The long blinks...' Wolfboy demonstrates. His eyes are an amazing arctic blue, and his lashes are criminally long.

'Why would you fight it?' I love sleeping. Going to work straight from school and trying to write essays afterwards has something to do with it.

'Because it's terrifying.' Wolfboy's face darkens. Honestly, it's like a cloud has parked over his head. 'Every time I go to sleep I don't know if I'm going to wake up again.'

I'm about to take him to task on this weird statement when I sip my drink and almost spray the entire mouthful. There must be at least four limes in this thing. Silver-hair is still watching us though, so I force myself to swallow, and raise my glass appreciatively in his direction. It's a beautiful piece of acting, if I do say so myself.

I lean back into my chair and watch the cold front pass over Wolfboy, catching him in an unguarded moment. He wouldn't look quite so wolfish if he wore his hair shorter and shaved more often. Not that I'm complaining. I love that bit in *King Kong*, the black-and-white 1930s version, when Fay Wray's clasped in King Kong's hairy fist at the top of the Empire State Building. Doesn't everyone secretly want to be in the clutches of a big animal? Or is that just me? I'm not sure it would work in my case, though. I'm not little and blonde like Fay Wray.

'So, what's so interesting about this place?'

Wolfboy leans forward and lowers his voice. 'That guy who bought us drinks? Well, I don't know him and I doubt he knows my band either.'

The drink gets better once I'm used to it, especially if I don't let it sit in my mouth for too long.

'People like knowing Locals. It gives them cred. Waving at me will probably get that guy laid tonight.'

'Locals…people who live in Shyness?'

'Yeah. They're easy to spot. You look for the moon tan.' Wolfboy looks around the room. He points carefully, with his hand held low at his waist. 'See those two over there? The girl with the curly hair and the guy with the goatee?'

I follow his finger. The girl with the curly hair is a porcelain doll in army pants. Goatee guy looks half drowned in an oversized black jumper. Their skin is so luminous I can see spidery blue veins just below the surface, even from this distance.

'Now check out this group over here.'

Two couples in their mid-thirties sit at a round table.

The women are skinny, pale and dressed in black. The men are pretty much the same, but have shorter hair. One of the women sees me watching her and stares back, a smile playing at the corners of her mouth. She knows I'm under-age for sure. The alcohol buzzes around my body. This place is getting stranger and stranger.

'No moon tan, but a whole lot of make-up and designer clothes. They're the converted warehouse crowd. They pretend they're doing it tough on the dark side of town, but they don't cross Grey Street, not even if their pure-bred wolfhound runs across the road and pisses on a homeless person.'

It's no wonder I can't read this place. There are different rules around here, things going on that I know nothing about. This must be what it feels like to be in a foreign country: confused and excited and unsure all at the same time. I shift in my seat and feel the sharp edges of the bankcard dig into me.

'I found something in the bathroom,' I say.

Wolfboy leans forward, interested for a millisecond before he is distracted by something over my shoulder. Or someone.

A woman stands at the foot of our table, her head tilted at just the right angle to set her shiny hair swinging around her face. A skintight catsuit the colour of gunmetal zips all the way from her bellybutton to her throat. She is teeny-tiny and beautiful and I desperately want to look exactly like her.

'Jethro.' She smiles at Wolfboy and ignores me. 'I knew it was you.'

Jethro?

'Jethro?' I say out loud.

The woman turns to me. Her hair cups her ears in a smooth Louise Brooks bob. 'I've never gotten used to calling him Wolfboy.'

Wolfboy doesn't return the smile. 'Wildgirl, this is Ortolan. Ortolan, Wildgirl.'

5

Ortolan joins us at our table, pulling up a leather cube that I'd assumed was decoration, not a seat. When I look at her closely I realise that she's the woman from the powder room. She perches on the cube with a cocktail in her hand. Her waist is so small I could circle it with my hands. What kind of name is Ortolan?

'How have you been, Jethro?'

Wolfboy pushes back in his chair and crosses his arms, tense from the tip of his boots to the top of his hair. 'Good.'

'How's the band going?'

'Good.'

'Have you played any gigs recently?'

'Nope.'

Ortolan nods like Wolfboy's said something really interesting. I look from her to him and back. I'm getting a weird feeling, like…Ortolan seems too old for Wolfboy, but who knows what goes on in this place? I finish my drink in one face-puckering gulp. Maybe it wasn't just my weak bladder that brought us here tonight.

'How's the shop going?' Wolfboy looks around the room like he doesn't care about her answer.

'It's going well. I'm always busy, so that's a good thing.'

There's another awkward pause. Ortolan's smile slips as she plays with the stem of her glass in lieu of conversation. I feel sorry for her all of a sudden. She's making an effort, which is more than I can say for Wolfboy. What's gotten into him?

'What sort of shop do you have?' I ask. Ortolan's eyes are the same grey as her catsuit.

'I design clothes.'

'Wow.' No wonder she looks so great. 'Is this one of yours?' I point at her outfit. If I had her body I'd get around in skintight lycra too.

Ortolan nods. 'Don't be too impressed. It's only a small shop, and I sew everything myself. Are you from the city, Wildgirl?'

To her credit she says my ridiculous alias without a hint

35

of sarcasm. But it seems like one thing for Wolfboy to call me Wildgirl, and another to hear it from the mouth of an adult. I blush.

'Is it that obvious?'

'It's a compliment. I'd kill to have gorgeous skin like yours.'

'Yeah, everyone around here looks like they could stand to eat a steak or two.'

Ortolan's laugh seems genuine. 'To be honest, I find this place a little pretentious, but I meet a lot of my customers this way. I have some regular clients who invite me out, and it's good to say yes sometimes.'

'They're kind of stare-y though. I feel like I'm on display.'

'They envy your youth. You two are like exotic creatures from the land of the young.'

I've never understood all that these-are-the-best-years-of-your-life crap. If this is as good as it gets then I might as well quit now. Let me get to the shimmery oasis of adulthood.

'What a joke.'

'They don't remember how confusing life was when they were your age.'

I'd almost forgotten about Wolfboy and his sulks, but he's obviously bored or irritated by our conversation because he stands up suddenly, all agitated and mumbly. Ortolan glances up in surprise.

'Excuse me, I gotta—I'm gonna—'

He walks off without finishing his sentence. Ortolan puts her empty glass down on the coffee table. Her eyes glisten like a road after rain. A silence spreads that doesn't seem like it's going to be filled by anyone but me. I have to ask. 'Is this an ex thing?'

'No.' Ortolan blinks her tears back. I'm relieved. If this is the sort of woman Wolfboy goes out with, I don't have a chance. That seems like all she's going to say, but I must look confused enough for her to feel like she has to explain. 'Sort of. I used to go out with Wolfboy's older brother. A long time ago.'

'Is that all? That's no reason to be so rude.'

'Don't be too hard on him…It was a difficult situation. Whenever I see Jethro, I always think for a split second that it's his brother. I'm always glad to see him, but…'

I crane my neck, trying to find Wolfboy. I spot him at the bar, talking to the guy who bought us drinks. As long as he doesn't leave without me. I turn to Ortolan again; her face is still pale with sadness.

'So you grew up in Shyness as well?'

'I did. But I left in my twenties and lived overseas for a few years. I moved back when I heard about the Darkness.'

'You moved back here? To live in the dark?'

'Well, close enough. I live just over the border, here in

37

Panwood. Everyone thought I was crazy to return. I can't explain it, but I knew I had to come back. It was the right thing to do.'

I can't imagine wanting to return to Plexus. Once I leave I won't come back until I've become something. A different person who won't get trapped there ever again.

'And you're a success here. I mean, you have your own shop. That must be so cool.'

'I don't think I could make the same clothes in another place. If I need inspiration all I have to do is walk the streets. You should drop by my shop sometime. I've got some pieces that would be great on you.'

'I'd like that,' I reply, meaning it. On first sight I thought Ortolan would be cold and aloof, but I couldn't have been more wrong about her.

Ortolan slides a phone out of a pocket I hadn't even noticed at her waist.

'Sorry, I'm just seeing if the babysitter's called.' She flips her phone open. 'No. I'm imagining things.'

'You have a kid?' I can't help sounding surprised. Ortolan laughs as if she's used to that reaction.

'A daughter. I don't leave her alone at night much so I'm a bit anxious. She's the reason I live over the border, not in Shyness proper. Do you want to see a photo?' Her face is alive. I can't imagine my mum's face ever lighting up like that when she talks about me. Ortolan passes me her open wallet.

Her daughter poses with a cardboard sword in one hand and a torch in the other. She wears a too-big tunic and a lumpy foil helmet. Her expression is halfway between goofy grin and ferocious battle-face. I remember playing dress-ups when I was little. I would spend hours making different costumes and acting out scenes with my soft toys.

'She's adorable. What's her name?'

'Diana.'

A shadow drops across the table.

We both look up at Wolfboy looming over us. His eyes are dark, and I follow his line of sight to the photo of Diana. Wolfboy's face twists and he seems on the verge of speaking, but instead he steps back and kicks out hard at the coffee table, turning it upside down with a crash. He pauses for a moment, looking as shocked as we are, then turns and runs.

six

I hit Grey Street running, boots bashing concrete, blood hammering in my skull. The gutter nearly trips me, I'm so desperate to get away. I'm choking, spitting clouds of breath, and not because of the running. A howl nearly forces its way past my lips and I have to bite hard to keep it down.

The toilet and the blazing convenience store lurch into view. The light sears my eyeballs. They must be tapping. No one has that much legal electricity.

I need darkness.

I leave them alone for one minute and Ortolan has to tell Wildgirl every little detail of her life.

Welcome shadows beckon on the next side street. The

memorial gardens are further along, down the slope that rolls all the way to the river. Orphanville sits to the right. The high-rise buildings are scattered with lights. My steps gradually slow until I find a vacant lot.

I sit on gravel and clumps of dead grass, digging my fingers into the stones and feeling dirt clog under my fingernails. I'm motionless now but my insides still race. I drink the night air in, taking each breath down as deep as I can, trying not to shudder. It gets colder in Shyness when it's night all over the City, even if it can't get any darker here. It's not fair that Ortolan would show Wildgirl a photo of her kid when I haven't even met her. Did they talk about Gram as well?

Gradually my blood cools, my heart slows. The Darkness is a heavy blanket that keeps me hidden from view.

I slip my hand inside my pocket and clutch my lighter, shutting my eyes as if I'm making a wish. The metal is cold and smooth against my fingers. Sometimes I think Lupe is right: my brother isn't far away. I can see him clearly if I concentrate. Out he comes from the darkness, sharpening quickly. Scruffy hair, an eagle tattoo on his bicep. He's leaning against his Valiant smoking, squinting into the bright sunlight. He flicks his cigarette butt onto the ground: *Let's go, Little J.*

The gravel crunches. My eyes snap open. At the far edge of the lot there's a patch of pink in the darkness, and two white legs. A pair of black boots walk towards me.

Wildgirl moves carefully. Her eyes are big, too big. She stands at a distance, using her bag as a shield.

'Hi.'

'How did you find me?' I sound pissed off. What I should be doing is apologising, but the right words aren't coming.

'I asked a few people. You're pretty distinctive so you weren't difficult to find.'

'Did you get chucked out of the bar?'

'No. We pretended it was an accident. The table wasn't even broken.'

That was lucky. I kicked it like I was trying to send it to the other side of the room. Wildgirl doesn't move any closer. I've scared her. I scare even myself when I get like that.

'Is Ortolan mad?'

'No. She's worried about you, though. She told me to come after you.'

I don't know what to say. The evening is teetering on the edge of failure. I don't want Wildgirl to go home, but I wouldn't blame her if she did. I can't bring myself to ask her to stay. Getting angry and then grovelling about it won't help. She doesn't seem like the kind of girl who'd stand for that.

'It doesn't bother me that you got upset. I don't need to know why. I just need to know that you're…safe. I'm taking a risk here. Same as you are with me.'

'I'm not dangerous. I don't kill cats for fun, if that's what you're asking. I don't bite people either.'

Wildgirl's face relaxes a little. 'Unless they ask nicely, right?'

My eyebrows knit. I'm always half a step behind her. I don't know why she's joking with me after what happened. I don't believe her when she says she doesn't need to know why I got upset. Maybe Ortolan already told her. I swallow. I don't want to talk about this stuff; I don't even want to think about it.

'We got off to a bad start,' I say. I push away the feeling that it would be easier to send her home.

'I still want you to show me around Shyness.'

Wildgirl comes closer and sits near me, her handbag next to her. She turns her hand over to show me something. A bankcard. She holds it out, gesturing for me to take it.

'I was about to tell you before Ortolan showed up. I found it in the bathroom at the Raven's Wing.'

The card isn't like any I've seen before, and I've never heard of FutureBank. It's been a while since I've seen a bankcard. I use cash and I get paid in cash, like most other Locals. There isn't a single bank branch left in Shyness.

'What do you think?' Wildgirl's voice is anxious.

'If we're banking on the future, then I'd say we're fucked.'

43

Wildgirl smiles. Her teeth are small and neat like breath mints. 'That was a good joke, Wolfie. You'd better watch it or I might think you have a sense of humour. What I meant was, do you think it works? Can we use it?'

'I guess so.' I turn the card over again in my hand. I can't see any reason why it wouldn't work. 'You didn't think to turn it in at the bar?'

'Haven't you ever asked yourself: what would I do with a million dollars?'

I try not to think about money too much if I can help it. I make some mixing other bands, and I've gradually sold off the best bits of furniture from my house. I know if I cross Panwood and go to the bank, which I do only if I'm desperate, someone, Mum probably, will have been topping up my account.

'Not really.'

'I do. I think about it a lot.' Wildgirl glows with excitement. 'Sometimes I start with ten thousand dollars, and then I work my way up to a million.'

'I doubt there's a million dollars in this account. Maybe this person's gone bankrupt and that's why they're leaving their card lying around.'

'Still, we should see if it works.'

I shrug. There's no name on the card anyway, so it would be difficult to find the owner. 'You'd better sign it then.'

Wildgirl finds a pen in her bottomless handbag and leans against my back to sign the card. I try to ignore the feathery touch of her hair against my neck. She's not scared of me anymore. When she's finished she squats in front of me.

'There's one more thing I have to ask you before we go any further.' Her cheeks flush. 'Do you have a girl-friend?'

'What?'

'If I hang out with you tonight, am I, you know, going to get slapped by someone?'

I shake my head. I don't know whether to feel insulted or flattered.

'Okay.' Wildgirl stands up. Something has been decided between us. 'I'm not calling you Jethro, by the way. You're Wolfboy to me, and that's what I'm going to call you.'

It's fine by me. I don't like being called Jethro. It's my name from before the Darkness, before everything changed. A name used by my parents and other people who haven't moved on yet. There's no point wishing that life could be like it was before.

7

We walk quickly through the backstreets of Shyness, but not quickly enough to stop me from half freezing to death. I pull my cardigan tighter around me. Mum would kill me if she knew I went out tonight without a jacket. It's amazing how she worries about small things like that, but never notices the big stuff.

I'm glad I found Wolfboy. I was more worried about him than I was about walking the mean streets on my own. I'm not surprised he's got some heavy personal history. When he howled in the pub, the sound cut right through me. It made me think about every miserable thing I've ever seen, like when you see a lost toy on the footpath, getting kicked along and muddied.

I glance across at him. He stares straight ahead as we walk in step, his handsome face composed again. It's already difficult to imagine that he's the boy I saw sitting in the empty lot just minutes ago, looking up at me as if he was drowning. It's difficult to imagine that he's the same boy I saw go ballistic and kick a table. Family stuff can do that to you. I'm the queen of losing my temper. If I was as tall as Wolfboy I would probably look just as scary as he did. I feel like we've passed some kind of test the night set us. I don't see what could go wrong from here.

Shyness isn't that different from Plexus, on the surface. The narrow houses crowd together. People grow couches and bikes and concrete in their front gardens instead of roses. The shabby comfort is familiar.

'You're taking me to an ATM, right?'

'No need. I've got enough money to last all night. For hours, I mean.'

'That's not the point though. I've got this card and I'm itching to blow some cash.'

'How are you going to use an ATM when you don't know the PIN for the card?'

I slap my forehead. A PIN. I must be cracking up. My face burns with the revelation that I'm a prize idiot.

'Can I just say in my defence that everything is really confusing in this place, and I don't normally drink whatever that foul thing was we drank at the Raven's Wing, and—'

'Don't worry about it.' Wolfboy dismisses my embarrassment with an easy wave of his hand. 'I have an idea where we can spend some plastic.'

'Where?'

'Somewhere top secret.' Wolfboy raises his eyebrows. Some of my dramatic tendencies must be rubbing off on him. I don't mind that he's got troubles—in fact, there's nothing worse than someone who's too happy-clappy—but I'm glad his mood isn't as black now.

The residential area gradually morphs into a semi-industrial area with super-sized buildings. We pass an autoshop, a fruit wholesaler and a ghost-town bus depot. The wider road and larger gaps between the buildings allow the wind to rush through, blowing dust and litter around our ankles. Shyness must be chock-full of opium dens, and illegal casinos and uh, diamond merchants and—I run out of ideas on places to spend dirty money. If we were in the City, well, I could think of a million ways. Wolfboy stops at a plain brick building with a neon skittle sign.

'We're going bowling?' I can't keep the disappointment out of my voice. Bowling is not badass. The foyer of the bowling alley is dark, even though one of the doors swings open and shut in the wind. 'Are you sure this place is open? I'd rather go to the skate rink if we're exploring lame entertainment options.'

'Be patient.' Wolfboy gives me an exasperated look. People are always telling me I talk too much. I vow to keep my mouth shut for a few minutes.

Instead of walking up to the main doors we take the laneway next to the building. A sprawling, multicoloured piece of graffiti covers the whole side wall: *KIDDS RUSH IN*. Someone forgot to use spell-check. Our footsteps are echoey in the quiet lane. Wolfboy keeps scanning the roofs on either side of us like he's expecting a masked invader to come swinging in on a rope. I slip my hand into Wolfboy's and he gives it a comforting squeeze.

The alleyway expands into a parking lot bordered by a row of unlit buildings with spindly fire escapes. A single weak streetlight illuminates the lot. The whole area is so deserted I expect tumbleweeds to barrel through the middle of it any second now. I swallow. Sketchy is good, right?

'I think it's somewhere near here.'

We cross the lot hand-in-hand. The last hand I held was probably Mum's, before I was old enough to be embarassed by it. My fingers burn and I hope my palm doesn't get sweaty.

'You don't even know where we're going?'

'I do know where we're going. That old guy at the bar,

49

the one who shouted us a drink, he was trying to impress me with all these underground things he knows about. He told me about this place and gave me directions. We're searching for a green door.'

'Like that one?' I point at the back of the building. A green door next to a mountain of glossy garbage bags.

Wolfboy drops my hand and presses the buzzer. The handwritten label below the button has smudged in the rain. Nothing happens. Wolfboy presses the buzzer again. Feet scuffle behind the door.

'We're looking for the market,' Wolfboy calls out, leaning in close to the door. I notice there's a surveillance camera above us, and try my best to look respectable. But maybe I should be trying to look shady instead?

The reply is muffled and terse. 'Password.'

Wolfboy whispers the password to the door, practically kissing the peeling paint.

'Can't hear you.'

Wolfboy rolls his eyes. 'PRINCE. OF. DARKNESS,' he repeats in a louder voice.

I snort.

The door clicks and swings inwards. We shuffle into a dark corridor. The owner of the voice is a tall thin man dressed like an oversized bat at a wedding. He doesn't look like an axe-murderer, but you never know.

'Your pass*word* is three words,' I say, to cover my nerves.

The man's glance is withering. He's wearing more eye make-up than I am and it's impossible to guess his age. His skin and his hair are exactly the same ivory-white. The concrete corridor is cold and unadorned; we're in the part of the building the public isn't meant to see.

'Who sent you?'

'Gary,' replies Wolfboy.

The man's face loses a little of its pinched look. Gary must be a favourite.

'I'm Sebastien.' He gestures with one crooked finger for us to follow him down the corridor, unlocking the door at the far end with a key strung around his neck. He makes us walk through first, before shutting the door behind us.

My eyes struggle to adjust to the gloom. I can make out a wall of shelves to the left, and something hanging from the ceiling. The only light comes from nine or ten small windows at floor level.

Sebastien's bodiless voice is as dry and papery as his skin. 'Welcome to the market. You will find I have a large variety of contraband and non-contraband items for sale. Please let me know if you have specialist needs and I will direct you to the appropriate section. I don't do sweets but I have an associate I can refer you to if that's what you're after.'

'I can't see anything,' I whisper to Wolfboy.

'Uh, Sebastien? Can we get some light in here, man?'

There's a dramatic sigh followed by several echoing footsteps. Sebastien clicks a cigarette lighter. He begins to light candles on a large candelabrum, his lacy cuffs swooping dangerously close to the flames. Wolfboy helps him, using his own lighter to spark the wicks. The room soon flickers with candlelight.

It's bigger than I anticipated. There are dozens of bicycles hanging overhead, shelves full of unlabelled tins, a stack of mattresses and an impressive collection of samurai swords and machetes pinned to the wall. Bins filled with various goods—sneakers, fireworks, lemon-shaped things that look like hand grenades—dot the room. If weapons are out in the open here, I wonder what 'specialist needs' Sebastien means.

'Do you take credit cards?'

'I'm not running a trash 'n' treasure here, darling,' Sebastien replies. 'Naturally I have card facilities. This *is* the largest black market operation in Shyness. I have a higher turnover than all the other so-called markets combined.'

Wolfboy wanders over to some shelves and picks up a tin, sniffing it suspiciously. 'Gary said you had music gear.'

'In the far corner, to your left.'

Sebastien folds himself into an antique chair behind a

desk and snaps on a lamp, making a great show of picking up a book and ignoring us. Wolfboy saunters to the back corner.

I bend down to peer through one of the floor-level windows. On the other side is a long, brightly lit room with matchstick people at the other end. The proportions are all wrong, as if I'm squinting into a diorama. I blink. It's not until there's a low rumble and something rolls towards me that I realise I'm looking into the bowling alley from behind the pins.

When I reach the back of the room Wolfboy is staring so reverently up at a wall of guitars that I don't want to interrupt his moment.

'Oh man.' He whistles through his teeth. 'He's got a Les Paul Custom.'

'A whatty-whatsy?'

The guitars all look the same to me, with only slight variations in shape and colour. Wolfboy leans forward and strokes a black guitar like it's a thoroughbred horse. It rocks lightly on its hook. Is it possible to be jealous of a guitar?

'A 1957 Gibson Les Paul Custom. Isn't she beautiful?'

She looks like a guitar to me. A black guitar with strings and the things that hold the strings in place, and those knobby bits at the end of the neck. I watch Wolfboy look at the guitar, his yearning painted all over his face.

It's pretty adorable, even though I'd prefer he look at me like that instead.

'Well, let's buy it. We're here to spend money, aren't we?'

'I already have a guitar.'

'Yeah, but you don't have *that* guitar. How much do they go for?'

'No.' Wolfboy turns away. 'I don't deserve a guitar that good. I don't play well enough.'

'That's ridiculous—' I begin but Wolfboy holds his hand up in my face.

'Not everything is an opportunity for an argument, young lady.'

I slap his hand away, smiling at his teacher voice. I walk along the wall, stroking the instruments as I pass them.

'Maybe I'll buy one and join your band.'

'Can you play the guitar?'

'That's not important, is it? I've got the right look for it.'

I stop at a collection of ukuleles. There's an awesomely ridiculous hot-pink one that's only fifty dollars. I pluck it from the wall and strum experimentally. Wolfboy leans against a bin full of headphones with his arms crossed, expectant. I clear my throat.

I don't know any chords, so the sound I'm making is admittedly terrible. But enthusiasm has got to count for something, right? I croon along to my discordant strumming, making the words up as I go.

Oh, I'm so lonely in the night
I'm so hairy
There's no light
I got the Shyness blues
I wear high-heeled shoes
The moon shines so bright
I'm so howly in the night

Time for the big finale. I thrash the ukulele for all it's worth.

Pants! So! Tight!
End-less-night!
Aa-woooooooh!

I attempt a howl but it comes out sounding more like a yodel. I compensate with some cock-rock thrusting and a few signs of the horns, before bowing.

Wolfboy claps slowly. He is devastatingly impressed, of course. More importantly, he seems to have forgotten all about the Ortolan business that got him so down in the first place. He is so sweet when he smiles. I want to see him do it more.

55

'Is that an original?'

I put the ukulele down and brush the hair off my face.

'Oh no, that's a cover of one of yours. You didn't recognise it?'

We grin at each other. I feel genuinely silly, not like earlier at the pub with Neil and Rosie when I was just doing a really good job of acting like I was having a good time. Wolfboy seems to like me acting the fool. That's good. I'm no stand-there-and-look-pretty kind of girl, and I'm not interested in anyone who wants that.

'So am I in? Do I make the cut?'

'You can be in my band any day. But we'd better get a move on, before Sebastien throws us out for being drunk and disorderly.'

Sebastien glances up as we approach his desk. He doesn't give any sign that he's heard anything. Out of nowhere my heart thumps like it's trying to break out of my chest. Time to test the card. I don't know if I'm feeling sick or excited.

'A good choice,' Sebastien says dourly as I hand him the pink ukulele.

'And this as well.' Wolfboy holds up a guitar strap. I didn't see him pick it up.

'Sixty-five dollars, please.'

I rub the card between my fingers for good luck, and

hand it to Sebastien, who swipes it straight through his machine, moving with bored efficiency.

Nothing happens. I hold my breath. I glance at Wolfboy and he is calm. His eyes, navy in this light, hold mine a moment longer than necessary and our secret passes between us.

The machine chirps and spits out a receipt.

Sebastien hands me a pen and I sign the slip of paper with a nervous hand. The card works. Part of me expected it to be a fake.

'Thanks, man.' Wolfboy hands me the ukulele and salutes Sebastien, who inclines his head a few degrees and returns immediately to his book.

My feet take me out the first door and down the corridor. I'm shaking all over. I know what I'm going to do with the card. I push on the outer door in a daze, barely registering the cold air rushing in to meet me. Tomorrow I'll go to a travel agent and buy myself a plane ticket, somewhere, anywhere. I won't have to go to school on Monday. I won't have to go back ever again. The card is my way out of the mess I'm in.

The parking lot is still deserted. Wolfboy takes the ukulele out of my hands and fixes the strap to it. He's got those blunt fingertips that boys have, but his hands are nimble. He pulls the strap over my head and under one arm so that the ukulele hangs against my back. I stand

57

still and don't breathe. Everything is going to be different from now on.

'We've got a name for people like Sebastien.' His hand lingers on my shoulder, straightening out the strap. He didn't exactly leap on me after I asked if he had a girlfriend. Doesn't he know what that question means?

'Yeah?'

'We call them "mushrooms" because they do well in the dark. Some people have made whole businesses out of the Darkness.'

'Like Ortolan?'

His hand drops off my shoulder. Damn. I shouldn't have mentioned her name.

'I guess. I've never thought of it like that, but yeah.' He pats me on the arm. A friendly pat. 'Let's get out of here. Are you hungry?'

eight

Saturnalia Avenue is dead as usual. The sight of Orphanville at the end of the street is enough to keep most people away. The trees lining the avenue are nothing more than dead wood in the ground. Every few weeks or so a branch breaks and crashes to the footpath, taking out anything or anyone in its way.

The dark is thick in this part of Shyness. The street is concrete, not tarmac, and is shot through with hundreds of cracks and potholes. No one bothers to fix roads anymore, or traffic lights or street signs. My body pushes against the Darkness, as if I'm wading through deep water. Even Wildgirl is silent.

Mostly Dreamers live around here. They're not scared

to live near Orphanville; the Kidds have no business with them. The Dreamer houses are paper cutouts, with balconies and lace and decorated roofs. Push the midnight silhouettes and they'd all fall over.

Thom and I broke in to a Dreamer house once. We found a broken window and laid our shirts over the jagged glass so we could climb through. We walked around the entire house without saying a word. There was no furniture, or light fittings, or mirrors, or carpets. Only bare floorboards and cobwebs, a wooden staircase leading upstairs, and dust everywhere. There was a bed on the first floor, in one of the smallest rooms. A couple of sofa cushions covered in twisted sheets as if the occupant had left in a hurry.

I have only one reason to come to this part of town, and that's to visit Lupe. Everyone knows Lupe and her van. People go to her for the best kebabs in Shyness, and to get answers to their questions. Even before the Darkness my parents warned me not to speak to her, but after Gram died the pull was too strong. Lupe told me things I wanted to hear. It didn't matter to me if they were true or not. She told me Gram wasn't far away at all, just on the other side of a curtain. That was before the Darkness, or before we realised the Darkness was coming. Sometimes I think the sun must have started failing around the same time that Gram left us.

I quicken my steps. I'm anxious to see Lupe's van shining in the night like a carnival ride. Lupe is definitely on my list of must-do's in Shyness. I know instinctively that Wildgirl will like her. And now that I've had the idea of food, I can't think of much else.

'Look,' whispers Wildgirl, leaning into me, spooked. It's a moment before I spot him.

A man stumbles along the road, about fifty metres off, walking towards us. He's got a classic Dreamer walk, dragging each leg after the other, hovering in mid-stride. His jumper sleeves hang as if he has no arms.

'Dreamer,' I explain. 'It's like a cult around here. All they want to do is sleep and dream. When they start out they take lots of pills so that they can sleep longer and dream more. But after a while they don't need the drugs: they can sleep for as long as they like. They're convinced that dreams are the true reality.'

The Dreamer passes us without seeming to register that we're here, his gaze fixed somewhere on the horizon. He barely has any colour at all, like he's been through the wash too many times. A lost soul. Wildgirl cranes her neck to keep watching him.

'You can't blame them, can you? You can do anything you want in your dreams, be anything you want to be. When you're asleep anything can happen, anything can be fixed, or reversed.'

She speaks like someone who's tamed her dreams. 'You should hear some dreamer-rock. It sends even me to sleep.'

Wildgirl still walks close, and it gives me an excuse to slip my arm around her shoulder.

'What are you going to do with the card now that you know it works?'

'I'm going to get on a plane and fly somewhere far, far away.'

'Where will you go?'

'Uh, India, I guess. Maybe.'

The only things I know about India are that it's crammed full of billions of people all trying to find some space, and that the sun would fry me in thirty seconds flat.

'Do you have family there?'

'Why would you say that?' Wildgirl is brittle all of a sudden.

'I don't know. You look like you're half-something.' Crap. She glares at me. 'It's…your hair is so dark, and your skin…'

Wildgirl pulls out from under my arm. 'Why don't you ask my mum? She says she doesn't know, but personally I think she's just holding out on me.'

I've ruined the moment.

When I was younger I used to imagine what it would be like if I had different parents. It had to be a mistake

62

that I got the ones I did. I was nothing that my parents wanted me to be. Neither was Gram, but I didn't think it bothered him as much.

Wildgirl should know that two parents are not necessarily better than one.

'My parents were some of the first to leave Shyness when things got difficult. My dad wants nothing but comfort and money. He wants all the dirt and noise in the world to be kept out of his house. He makes all the rules, but he's soft. He never lifts a finger, except to send emails.' I strike a body-builder pose. 'Looks like Mum was secretly running with the pack.'

Wildgirl smiles. She knows what I'm trying to do. She grabs me and turns me around, pointing at the ghostly Dreamer, floating into the darkness.

'See that guy? Half-zombie for sure.'

We're almost at Lupe's van. There are no trees at all in this part of Saturnalia Avenue. The Kidds probably used them for one of their bonfires.

'Kidds Rush In,' says Wildgirl, as if she's reading my thoughts.

'What?' I'm startled.

She points at a billboard pasted to the side of an old milk bar. The poster is bright and fresh compared to the pocked brick wall underneath. *Doctor Gregory Cares*, it says along the bottom edge. Doctor Gregory's tanned face smiles above the slogan. He has suspiciously white teeth.

Doctor Gregory Cares about money, if you ask me.

Someone has spray-painted three letters across Doctor Gregory's face. Monkey writing, wobbly and uneven.

'*K. R. I.* Just like the graffiti near the bowling alley. Kidds Rush In.'

She's sharper than I thought. Or less drunk. I'm even more impressed by her ukulele performance in that case.

Wildgirl steps towards the billboard. 'Who are the Kidds?'

Before I can reply a small dark shape drops from the sky and lands on Wildgirl's head. Long, furry fingers reach for her eyes. To her credit Wildgirl doesn't scream, but thrashes from side to side, the ukulele bouncing on her back. The animal loses its grip on her hair, falls to the ground and scampers off. I rush to Wildgirl's aid, but she pushes me away, pointing behind me.

I turn around and there they are—the Kidds.

Five of them spread out in a semicircle in front of us, their bikes thrown to the ground behind them. If I'd been concentrating on our surroundings, rather than making Wildgirl smile again, I would have heard their wheels long before they got here. I recognise the tallest Kidd instantly, a guy known as the Elf. The Elf is weedy, with lank blond hair and skin the colour of uncooked dough. Flanking him are two boys and two girls of varying ages. One girl has her hand in her pocket, which probably means a knife. They all have plastic police tape tied around their heads like sweatbands.

The Elf pushes the littlest Kidd forward. He can't be more than seven. There are drool streaks down the front of his too-big basketball top.

'Tell them, Baby.'

'Give us your bag!' Baby demands in a reedy voice. 'You holding. We know it.'

Wildgirl laughs. I don't blame her. Baby barely reaches her waist. The tarsier sits on Baby's shoulder now, licking its paws and chattering, baring a mouth full of holey teeth. I was slack. I should have asked Wildgirl if she was carrying. A bag that big, there has to be something.

'Run back to Mummy, little boy.'

'Monkey don't make mistakes.' Baby huffs and grimaces, working himself up into either a tantrum, or a fit of tears. His headband dangles in his eyes. He looks to the Elf for guidance.

'Listen, you cola-colour City chick'—the Elf forces his words out slow, when anyone can see he's high as a kite—'hand over the bag. And give Baby some respect.'

The Kidds are restless, shuffling and twitching. I wonder who would come to the Elf's aid if I jumped on him and made him shut his big mouth. The third boy, a Kidd around twelve, appears stoned out of his brain and won't be a problem. He wanders around, kicking aimlessly at the road. Knife-girl seems like the only other fighter among them and is probably second-in-charge. The problem is, Wildgirl doesn't know that no one messes with the Elf, no matter what he calls you. She starts swinging her bag at Baby.

'I'm. Not. Giving. You. Fucking. Little. Brats. Anything.'

Baby ducks and swerves, but he stays fixed on Wildgirl.

'You got a nightmare mouth, girl.' The Elf almost sounds impressed, but I see him move his fingers down low, waving the knife-girl forwards. 'If you was Local I might ask you to join my crew.'

'Give it to him,' I tell Wildgirl in a flat voice.

She gapes at me. 'What?'

'Hand over your bag. They're not going to take what you think they're going to take.'

'Good dog.' The Elf stares at me with midnight eyes. I feel a wave of heat rising from my stomach. If I was on my own I'd be sorely tempted to take him on. I've lost track of the other boy and girl. I turn to find them both standing behind me, within striking distance.

'Get any closer and I'll thump you,' I tell them. I don't have to raise my voice. I'm ten feet tall when I'm pissed off.

'Ooooh.' The girl purses her lips, pretending to be

scared. The boy giggles at something only he can see.

Wildgirl hands her bag to Baby. You can tell she hates doing it. Baby puts the bag on the ground and rifles through it with sticky, dirty fingers. Baby needs a bath. I can smell him from here. He skips over Wildgirl's phone and wallet, and pulls out a packet of gum, a bag of jelly-beans and a blister pack of throat lozenges, piffing them at knife-girl, who stuffs them down the front of her jumper with one hand.

Baby finishes ransacking the bag and kicks it along the ground to Wildgirl. He stands next to the Elf, fishing for approval that doesn't come.

I think that's it but then the Elf opens his mouth. 'Body search.'

The tarsier leaps off Baby's shoulder and is at Wild-girl's feet in a flash. She stares down at the animal in disgust. The tarsier places one paw on her foot and then the other. He fishes around inside the ankle of her boots and then climbs her legs, slowly. He sticks his long fingers in her shorts pockets and then climbs higher, feeling as he goes. Wildgirl stands still, but her legs are shaking. She's breathing audibly through her nose. I follow her eyes to knife-girl, who has taken her blade out of her pocket and holds it up idly as if she's about to peel apples.

The tarsier finishes searching and finds nothing. He

scampers back to Baby, leaping effortlessly from the ground up to the Kidd's shoulder.

'Thank you for doing business, boys and girls.' The Elf smirks and backs away to his bike. I scoop Wildgirl's bag up from the ground.

'I don't know why you bother with the small stuff,' I say, belatedly. When the Elf doesn't respond I put my arm around Wildgirl and lead her away.

9

I feel safe finally in Guadal-
upe's van, which is as pink as the inside of a watermelon
and as crammed full as a caravan could be. I feel like a
marionette with its strings cut; my legs are shaking so hard
I barely made it up the steps. I know Wolfboy could have
run here much faster, but held back for me.

Guadalupe is a big woman in a psychedelic tent-dress.
She's got tomato-coloured hair and smudged coral lipstick,
but her eyes are bright and shrewd. She looks crazy, but I
know instantly that she's not. When I hold my hand out
to shake hers, she flips it over and traces the inside of my
arm with glossy purple fingernails.

'Just kebabs, Lupe.' Wolfboy pulls my arm away from

her and stands between us. It all seems a bit protective, especially since it was his idea to come here. Not that I was planning on just standing around after the gang was done with us.

Lupe doesn't seem offended. She pats Wolfboy's shoulder like he's a big old poodle. They act like old friends. She doesn't even mind that he doesn't use her proper name.

'You're hungry then, my boy?'

'Always.' He sits down at a table that takes up one end of the van and gestures for me to join him. I pick up the pile of books already occupying the seat and try to find a bare surface to put them on. The best I can do is to balance them on some satin cushions. I slide into the narrow gap between the table and the horseshoe-shaped bench, sitting opposite him. I flap my t-shirt, trying to dry the wet patches under my arms.

'I give you the bloody bits,' Lupe tells Wolfboy, 'just how you like.'

I make an *oh-really?* face at Wolfboy. He looks embarrassed and starts smoothing his hair into place. Impressive. It's still holding its shape, even with all the running.

'And you, my darling? Are you hungry?' Lupe's accent is from somewhere else; she speaks so lazily, the word 'darling' comes out as *daaaahhhlink*.

'Yes, please.' Now that I think about it my stomach twinges with hunger and a headache dances at the edges of my vision. 'But no bloody bits,' I add. I was too busy glamming up after work to eat any dinner. There was nothing in our fridge anyway, and I couldn't be bothered walking to the shops. No wonder I got so tipsy earlier.

Even with all the clutter, the van is much bigger inside than the outside suggests. I can't see a bed so the table must fold down to make one. Lupe is visible through the beaded curtain that separates her living quarters from the kitchen. She tinkles through the curtain now and places a cup and saucer in front of me.

'To make things better' is all she says, before returning to the kitchen. Wolfboy nods so I sip the tea. It's hot and sour and the colour of green apples. If it's witchcraft, I'm not complaining because calm rolls over me almost instantly. My heart returns to normal, and my legs stop burning.

I examine the van. The walls are quilted in pink vinyl and studded with crystal buttons. A sideboard crammed with photos, statues and crockery runs down one side of the van, opposite the door; above that shelves groan with books and LPs. There's some seriously crazy shit in here: a grinning skull on a stick, a string of lights in the shape of lotus flowers, a bunch of dried chillies hanging in one corner, peacock feathers in a vase, a case of pinned butterflies, a rusty microscope, jars of pickled god-knows-what.

I drink the last of my tea. Wolfboy has his head in his hands and seems unable to meet my eyes. The table is covered all over with photos cut out of old magazines, topped with a thick layer of varnish. I'm leaning on some of my favourite old-timey movie stars. Lupe has good taste when it comes to films. Maybe not so much on the interior decorating.

Lupe clatters plates and knives in the kitchen, and Wolfboy still doesn't speak. He looks exhausted, blinking those gorgeous blue eyes like it's the only thing he has energy left to do. I want to cradle his tired face in the palms of my hands.

'You've got the long blinks,' I tell him.

'Sorry,' he mumbles.

'For what?'

We're safe. I saw my first Dreamer. The bit where I got attacked by the Ewok was freaky, but I can hardly complain when freaky is what I've been demanding. And here I was worrying the night was going to be all ritzy bars and wankers. I'll tell you one thing: when I was running from those brats it was the only time I managed to forget what I've been trying to forget all day.

'That was my fault. I should have asked you if you were carrying. Are you okay?'

I touch my head all over to see if that nasty little animal actually drew blood with its claws. I still have my handbag

72

and my phone and my keys and the magic bankcard. I didn't dare check on the card until we were well out of sight. I haven't had a chance yet to think seriously about my travel plans but I have no intention of giving up this card for anyone.

I check under the table, and my tights aren't even ripped.

'I'm fine, really.'

I got rolled by a monkey and a bunch of kids on hotted-up bikes and they didn't take the one valuable thing I have on me. The kid who went through my bag was barely old enough for school, and he was terrified, his lower lip wobbling like he was going to burst into tears. I can see the funny side, but Wolfboy still looks shattered.

'I should have seen them. They would have been follow-ing us for a while.'

'The monkeys or the brats?'

'The monkeys. They're called tarsier. They're foot soldiers. They find targets, get information and follow people. They can go places no one else can. The one that attacked you would have dropped off a roof.'

The tarsier didn't look like any monkey I've ever seen. It was too small for one thing, and its bulging saucer-eyes took up almost its whole head, and it had huge hands with nubby fingers. I wish I could have a shower to get rid of the feeling of its filthy fingers brushing against my face.

'Such big eyes,' I say, and I'm not sure if I'm talking

73

about the kids or the monkeys.

'The night favours those with big eyes.' The words sound strange coming out of Wolfboy's mouth, like he's reciting a proverb. 'Remember, if you see tarsier, the kids aren't far behind.'

Somehow, through my fatigue and hunger, a few pieces of the puzzle slide into place.

'Kids? Kids as in K-I-D-D-S rushing in, right?'

Wolfboy nods. The graffiti near Sebastien's makes more sense now.

'You were scared,' I say. 'We were outnumbered, sure, but none of them was older than fourteen or fifteen.'

'I'm sorry. I should've stepped in earlier. They had no right to search you like that…it was out of line. But I recognised the leader of that gang. A guy called the Elf. Everyone around here knows he's bad news.'

'I don't blame you,' I say, and I mean it. 'Were they really only interested in jelly beans?'

If he'd gone for the bankcard Baby would have received a good smack on the bum.

'The Kidds are sugar freaks, and they've got the tarsier hooked as well. They were all high, completely off their chops. You can tell when you look at their eyes.'

There *was* something weird about the way the Kidds moved; their eyes sliding and their hands twitching. There's plenty of junkies in Plexus, but none that young.

'Can sugar really do that to them?'

'In high enough doses, yeah. They'd do anything for it. Usually they don't bother with the small stuff, but maybe it's been a slow night. Or they were bored.' Wolfboy frowns. 'I shouldn't have let them search you.'

I want to reach across the table and put my hand over his, but Lupe tinkles through the curtain again and I fold my hands in my lap instead. The smell of meat and garlic wafts in. Lupe's face shines from the heat of the rotisserie.

'What are you thinking?' she asks abruptly, putting a plate in front of me.

'I'm thinking you have a lot of crap in here.'

God, that wasn't very polite. The woman invites us into her home and feeds us and I call her possessions 'crap'. Fortunately Lupe just laughs and squeezes into the seat next to me. Three is a tight fit, and none of us are small people. I tuck my feet on either side of Wolfboy's ankles, nudging him, but he doesn't seem to notice.

The kebab takes up the entire plate, a thick roll of pita bread stuffed with salad and meat and dripping with sauce. Wolfboy takes huge bites out of his like he hasn't eaten in several years. I take a quick look at his plate. Chunks of charred meat fall out of the bread. Nothing raw or bloody that I can see.

He catches me looking. 'It's cooked. I'm not an animal.'

'I didn't think—I know you're not…' I can't think of what else to say so I pick up my kebab and take a bite. It's delicious—salty and crispy and garlicky in all the right proportions. The bread falls apart in my hands but I just pick up the pieces and keep shovelling it in. I can't believe how hungry I am. We don't talk as we eat, and Lupe seems to enjoy watching us. I become human again with food in my stomach.

As soon as I finish my meal, licking my fingers clean and sighing with satisfaction, Lupe sits up abruptly, making the red beads around her neck dance.

'Darling, your arm.' Lupe takes my hand in hers again and stretches my arm out flat, so that the pale skin of my inner arm is exposed. 'I read skin,' she explains. 'Like palm reading, but instead I read your veins.'

'Lupe,' growls Wolfboy, pushing his plate away. There's colour in his cheeks now and life back in his eyes. He looks at me. 'You don't have to if you don't want to.'

My veins are barely visible.

'Have you had it done?' I ask him. He nods.

Up close Lupe's face is crisscrossed with powder-caked lines. I've never had my palm read, or my stars done, or seen a psychic. I don't think you can ask them to only tell you the good stuff and filter out the bad. I need to believe that good things are going to happen to me soon, to make up for all the crap that's been happening recently.

'You shouldn't be afraid,' says Lupe, 'I already see lots of life here.'

'Sure,' I say. I don't have to believe what she tells me anyway. Hopefully she'll say that I'm about to begin a long journey and leave all my problems behind. And if she doesn't then I'm strong enough to think otherwise.

Lupe begins to tap my arm lightly all over with her fingertips.

Wolfboy slides along the bench and frees himself from the table.

'I'll wait outside.'

I can't tell if he's pleased or upset that I've agreed to have my arm read.

'Is that safe?' I ask. 'Maybe you should stay. I don't mind.'

'There's a circle around the van,' Guadalupe says. 'A circle no one can enter without my say so.'

Wolfboy turns; our eyes meet before he leaves. The van dips as he steps down. The door clatters shut behind him.

I give Lupe a nervous smile as I shift in my seat. The familiar weight of my handbag rests on my feet.

Guadalupe's face slackens; only her eyes remain sharp. I watch her as she traces patterns over my arm. It's so relaxing sitting in this pink capsule, with my arm being stroked like there's a miniature figure skater gliding over it. I feel my breathing slow and my mind empty.

ten

There are changes that creep up on you slowly, and then there are sudden changes that rip you apart, so that you don't know who you are anymore. When I first visited Lupe, I had been ripped apart. I was so scared I thought my legs wouldn't carry me there. I was fourteen and no one knew the Darkness was on its way. Cars still drove down Saturnalia Avenue, and Orphanville was just an abandoned housing development.

That was back when the petrol station was still open and there were canvas flags strung around the forecourt, bags of ice in the big freezer out the front and gas bottles for hire. Lupe's van was newly painted. I'd heard all the stories about Lupe at school: that she was a witch, that she could see the future, that she could make bad things happen to people who'd done you wrong, that she could talk to the dead.

My parents warned me about her. I think they were scared of her because she was different. Fat women horrify my mum. She says they've let themselves go. My mum can't let anything go.

I find it difficult to remember now. Remembering involves being able to picture myself a few years ago, and that's almost impossible. I had a scrawny body and barely a hint of facial hair. For weeks I went to Lupe's van and barely spoke to her. I walked there full of purpose, but when I got there I froze and wound up eating my kebab under her canopy, miserable that I didn't have the guts to say anything.

Eventually, on maybe my fifth visit, Lupe handed me my change and asked, 'Is there anything else you want, my boy?'

The question stopped me dead. What did I want? I wanted things to be like before. No. Before was too long ago. Before I stopped talking to my parents, before Gram moved out and we hardly ever saw him, before Gram and Ortie split up. Before was when I was ten and we all lived in the one house, like a family. Before was impossible.

Really, I didn't know what I wanted. I stood there opening and closing my mouth like the dumb kid I was. Maybe I wanted to know why bad things happened. Or when the pain would stop.

In the end I didn't have to say anything. Lupe disappeared from her window and unlatched the door. I sat at her table, my arm laid out flat across the plain orange laminex. Lupe's van was a lot emptier back then. She read my arm in a trance. She said a lot of things, some of which I don't remember. Every now and then I'll have a flashback, and I'll be reminded of something she said. Things that meant nothing then have grown to mean something over the years.

'You must be careful not to get cut off,' she said. 'Don't go too far inside yourself.'

Maybe it's too late for that. She probably meant don't live on your own in a big house, rattling around the empty rooms. She probably meant talk to your friends about things that matter instead of filling in time drinking and listening to music.

There were other things. She said there was a black spot inside me, a blind spot. She said it worried her that I was keeping things hidden inside this spot, things that should really be let out.

It was Lupe who mentioned Gram first.

'Your brother has gone, but not too far. He left this

world, but there are other places very close by. He can still see you. He smiles.'

I could have asked: Why did he do it? How could he leave me? Why would he be smiling now when he was so unhappy before?

I don't believe in heaven so it's hard to believe in those other places Lupe talks about. But maybe it wasn't heaven she meant.

I sit on the tail of the caravan, using the spare tyre as a cushion. The fairy lights strung across Lupe's awning lift the gloom more than you'd expect; the light they give off forms a perfect circle around the van. Beyond that are dark patches where the petrol bowsers have been torn out, leaving holes in the concrete. I exhale, trying to blow away the heavy cloud of memories.

I was another person then.

I wonder what Lupe is saying to Wildgirl now.

You'll find yourself telling the truth in Lupe's van. That's what I should have told Wildgirl before we even stepped inside.

81

eleven

Wildgirl and I walk back up the concrete desert of Saturnalia Avenue, taking our time. The sound of our footsteps volleys between the houses. Lupe placed a protection on us before we left. I didn't ask her how it works. Presumably walking through the gates of Orphanville with a kilo of caster sugar is still out. But it was generous of Lupe, and it has made me relax a little. She always knows what I need, even if I don't. 'Enjoy yourself,' she said as we left the van. Then she whispered in a more serious voice, 'Stay close to her.'

Wildgirl is uncharacteristically silent. I haven't known her for long, but I do know that she doesn't mind shooting her mouth off. I like it that she says exactly what she's thinking, but right now her mind is somewhere else. I won't ask her what Lupe said or what she told Lupe. What goes on in Lupe's van is private. I thought I was doing the right thing taking Wildgirl there but I should have known Lupe would talk her into a reading. Lupe means well, but she doesn't exactly do small talk. I need to get Wildgirl out of whatever memory she's stuck in, and back with me.

'Uh, do you want to hear some of the crackpot theories?'

'What theories?'

'You know, theories for the Darkness. Everyone's got one.'

Wildgirl turns to me and manages a weak smile. I won't ask.

'Sure.'

'Here goes. Armageddon has already happened—even though no one remembers it happening—and we're living in hell. Of all the locations on earth that God could have chosen for hell, he chose Shyness.'

Everyone in Shyness knows these theories. We all get the leaflets. We all hear the godbods' megaphones blaring as they drive around in their salvation van. Wildgirl looks interested so I continue. 'The Darkness is punishment for our sins. Why it's only Shyness getting punished no one can say. I guess you have to believe that people living in

Shyness are bigger sinners than everyone else.'

'Well, I don't believe in sin or hell so neither of those works for me.'

Wildgirl is so damn sure about everything—that's another thing I like about her. There are a lot of grey areas in my life. I can't say for sure that the sun didn't fall because of something I did wrong.

'The government is trying to find a solution for global warming and they chose Shyness as the testing ground. They think if they can keep the earth in total darkness for a few years then it will cool down enough to reset the climate.'

'I like that one,' Wildgirl says. 'Anything involving government conspiracies and I'm into it.'

I've exhausted my theories. Paul's got a complicated one involving bio-responsive shields and aliens, but to be honest I barely understand it. But I've managed to drag Wildgirl back from where she was. I can tell she's actually seeing what's around her now: the streetlights and the abandoned buildings, and me.

'What do you want to do now?'

'I don't know. What do you want to do?'

Maybe we should do something quiet for a while. Something safe. We could listen to music at my house. Would it sound sleazy if I suggested going to my house?

'You know what I want to do? I want to go somewhere

really full-on, with loud music and lots of people, and I want to dance.' Wildgirl's face turns disco-ball bright. Talk about quick recoveries.

It wasn't what I was expecting but if that's what she wants then I know where to go. If Thom and Paul didn't show up at the Diabetic after we left, then they'll almost definitely be at Little Death instead. We need to cut back through Shyness, towards O'Neira Street. I text Thom, asking him where they are now and to get our names on the door at Little Death. Wildgirl thinks I'm a minor Shyness rock star and I'd hate to disappoint her. The downside of all this is that I'll have to introduce her to Thom and Paul. I'm not sure I want her to meet my friends.

We pass Quarrel's Alibi Agency and then I take us down the next street on the right. As we turn in to the darker side street, Wildgirl walks closer to me again. I reach down and take her hand, hoping my palms don't suddenly turn sweaty. Miraculously, she laces her fingers through mine, rather than shaking me off. I know she grabbed my hand earlier, but that was when she was scared. This wasn't as difficult as I thought it would be.

'Do you think they're still there?'

'Who?'

'The little tarsy things.'

'Maybe.'

Definitely. There's a dark speck on a nearby lamppost,

and a bobbing movement or two on a rooftop across the street. I doubt Wildgirl can see them though.

No one knows how the tarsier got to Shyness. There aren't many other places in the world you'll find them. They appeared around the time the Kidds got organised, and they've been here ever since. Everyone thinks they're dependent on the Kidds, but I'm not so sure. Tarsier are small and fast, and they see better than anyone or anything else in the dark. There are times when tarsier have jumped people and there hasn't been a Kidd in sight.

'So, who is Doctor Gregory anyway?' Wildgirl stops in front of a row of smashed-up vending machines. Cigarettes, water, night-vision goggles. None of them work anymore except for *Doctor Gregory's Solution*, which is lit up and intact. *Doctor Gregory's Solution* is similar in design to an old-style photo booth with a short curtain over the doorway. A large photo of the ubiquitous doctor decorates the outside. Four dollars for five minutes.

'The billboard guy again. Who is he?'

'He's a dickhead, that's what he is.'

'What sort? There are many different varieties.'

She's right. Doctor Gregory is a very specific sort of dickhead. He's built an empire on anxiety. He pretends he cares but really he wants things in Shyness to stay the same so he can keep making money.

'Doctor Gregory thinks that all kids have a problem

and bills himself as the man to fix them. For a price, of course.'

'Well to be honest, the Kidds I've met so far have been kind of fucked up.'

'Not all kids are like that. Doctor Gregory convinces parents that their children need to go on expensive sugar-replacement medications. Babies and toddlers and older kids who haven't joined the gangs—kids who don't really have a problem. They get as hooked on Doctor Gregory's medication as they would get on sugar. And that's not where it stops. He wants to medicate *everyone* in Shyness, adults included. For depression, light deprivation, having a bad hair day, anything. If he had his way we'd all be popping pills.'

I once received a letter from Doctor Gregory offering to cure me of my 'psychosomatic hypertrichosis'. I ripped it up and threw it in the bin. A week later this guy in a shirt and tie shows up on my doorstep, clipboard in hand, claiming to be doing market research for the local council. I sent him on his way. Now, I just keep putting the letters in the bin without reading them.

Wildgirl leans closer to read the small writing on the side of the booth. A manifesto-teaser. You have to pay for the full version: book, e-book, podcast or DVD, take your pick.

'So, Doctor Gregory is a mushroom then?'

'He's more like a toadstool.'

'I wanna go inside.'

I exhale loudly. It figures.

'Look, this might be old news to you, but this is *fascinating* to me.'

I have zero interest in stepping into Doctor Gregory's booth. Wildgirl sticks her head through the curtain. Her hand tugs on mine.

'He brainwashes people—'

Wildgirl hauls me into the booth before I can say more. She pushes me onto the swivel stool inside, and sits on my lap, leaning forward to put coins in the slot. The booth isn't designed for two people. Doctor Gregory suddenly becomes far more interesting.

'Are we concerned parents or disturbed yoof?' Wildgirl asks. I can't really speak with her squirming like this, let alone make any rational decisions. I lean back before I embarrass myself.

'Okay, we're disturbed yoof,' she decides without me, and pushes another button. In front of us are two speakers, a screen, a microphone and a chute. There's no point trying to keep my distance, because Wildgirl slumps into me as the screen flickers in front of us. All that's missing is the popcorn.

Doctor Gregory sits on a park bench in front of a cardboard set that's supposed to resemble a playground. His jeans are so high-waisted they're grazing his nipples.

Hello! Thanks for dropping in. I'm Doctor Gregory. Please touch the screen to take a diagnostic test.

'What do you want?' Wildgirl reads out the animated bubbles floating around the doctor. 'Bad Thoughts, Bad Deeds or Bad News?'

'Bad Thoughts.' Wildgirl is soft and hot and heavy against me.

The lights dim slightly and a single spotlight highlights Doctor Gregory's spray-tanned face.

Please answer the following questions honestly, stating your answers in a clear voice.

Do you often feel angry and out of control?

'Yes!' Wildgirl bounces up and down. 'Both. At the same time.'

Do you ever think that you are alone in the world and that nobody cares about you?

'Oh yeah, constantly,' I chime in, getting into the spirit of things. It's not that hard to do. Wildgirl's enthusiasm is infectious.

Do you ever steal things without knowing why?

Wildgirl flings her arms out, nearly hitting me in the face. 'Only hearts, baby!'

I can't argue with her on that one. Doctor Gregory leans forward, a penetrating expression on his orange face. He's really getting off on this.

Do you often have strange thoughts that disturb you?

'Yeah,' I say, 'I have unnatural feelings towards goats.'

Wildgirl titters.

I do not understand this answer. Please state your answer again in a clear voice.

'Yes, doctor,' Wildgirl says. 'GOAT LOVE.'

Doctor Gregory doesn't even blink. I guess bestiality is nothing in his line of business.

Do you have a big fear of the future?

This is too easy.

'I have a big fear of your jeans,' I manage to spit out. Wildgirl laughs so hard she nearly falls on the floor. Her laugh is more of a snort, and it's the hottest sound I've ever heard.

Thank you for completing the test. Please collect your diagnosis.

A slip of paper slides down the chute.

You have a borderline personality disorder. You must visit the Doctor Gregory Wellness Clinic for immediate treatment. You do not need parental permission to attend the clinic. Take the first step in your new life!

There's a piano-tinkle and then a woman warbles *Doctor Gregory Caaaaarreees!*

'Wow,' I say. 'We're really fucked up, aren't we?'

I'm thinking up a billion ways to stall Wildgirl so that we can stay in the too-small booth. She twists around to face me.

'I went to see a shrink for a while,' she says, in the same way someone might say 'How 'bout that moon today?' 'Mum made me.'

I notice for the first time that she's wearing this amazing necklace made of white feathers strung together. This means I'm looking down when I should be looking up. I look up.

'Why?'

'Oh, something about me having no friends.'

'What was it like?'

I love it that Wildgirl tells me that kind of stuff, straight up, like it's no big deal. Mum and Dad tried to make me see someone after Gram died but I refused. Lupe was right around the corner when I was having a bad day.

'It was all right.' She chews on her bottom lip. 'But it didn't work, because things are worse than ever.'

I can see every detail of her face. She's got a stray eyelash balancing on one cheek, but if I brush it off it will look like the worst sort of cliché. I think that there's more she wants to say but I could have it wrong. Maybe it's my turn to say something.

'Do you mean at school?' I ask eventually. 'Things are worse than ever at school? Or home?'

Wildgirl doesn't seem to hear me.

'Your teeth,' she says, with a funny little smile, 'are as big as tombstones.' She says it in such a way I know she doesn't mean it as a bad thing. She says it as if to say: that's all I'm telling you for now.

There's a pause so yawning I can't help but think about what it would be like to lean in and kiss her, but if I'm getting the signals wrong then I'm about to destroy the best run we've had all evening. It's been at least ten minutes since I've said or done anything stupid. The decision is taken out of my hands when my phone beeps loudly. Wild-girl laughs. I pull my phone out of my shirt pocket and it's Thom. He's sorted it out. They're at Little Death. We're in.

12

I'm the picture of nonchalance. I use this look a lot: when I'm handing in forged permission slips at school, when I come home three hours late, when I'm fooling around on the internet at work instead of calling clients, and when I'm pretending to be older than I really am. I had this same mask on at school today, pretending that I didn't care, while the whole time I felt as if my insides had been vacuumed out.

I lean on the counter, a big mistake because the beer mats in this club are so sodden you could grow grass on them. The counter is a long concrete slab, raised so the barman towers over me. 'I'll have a vodka raspberry and a pot, please.' I rustle in my wallet.

Of course I know exactly how I'm going to pay—with the card that's in my pocket—so there's no need to rummage in my wallet, but it's best to keep busy when you don't know if you're going to get served or not.

The barman sighs and places both hands on the bar. His spiky black hair wouldn't look out of place on a cockatiel.

'No raspberry. I can give you straight vodka, or vodka soda. What beer do you want?'

The way the barman talks you'd think he'd been serving drinks for hundreds of years instead of just a few hours. As if I know what beer Wolfboy wants. Or what beer they even serve in Shyness.

'You don't have tonic? Or orange juice?'

'We're strictly no-crose around here, babe.'

I don't like his smug face. No-crose? Whatever. I don't need another drink anyway. The whole night will be a waste if I wake up tomorrow and can't remember a thing. And if we come across any more Kidds I want to be alert, not drunk.

'Just a plain soda then, *honey*.' I hate being called 'babe'. I fish in my pocket for the card. 'Any beer, I don't care.'

The barman strops off and I lean against the bar, flipping the card over in my hands. The club is an impressive underground cavern with stone walls and a concrete floor polished smooth by thousands of feet. The main room has a stage and a dancefloor and the bar, but there are doorways and passages leading off everywhere. The far side of the main room is separated from pitch-black emptiness by a wire fence. Metal struts loaded with lights span the ceiling. The air throbs with distorted noise. It's hard to tell what's a shadow and what's a real, living, breathing person. A tall girl with whiter-than-white hair brushes past me. She's wearing a pair of black stockings as a top, crisscrossing the stretchy material over her shoulders and chest and tying the ends around her waist. I'll have to remember the trick; it looks awesome.

Wolfboy is still over by the door, where it's lighter, deep in conversation with two guys.

'Buy me a drink, lady?'

Someone tugs on my t-shirt. The speaker is either a very small boy with an old man's face, or a very small old man with a boy's voice. He smiles winsomely. Or it would be winsome if he had any teeth left.

'Buy me a drink?'

'Do I look like a charity?'

'Ohhh, go on.' The man-child wears a tweed golf cap; it doesn't hide the way his skin collects in unhealthy wrinkles around his mouth. He's wearing baggy pants and a waist-coat, like an extra from *Oliver Twist*.

'Aren't you up past your bedtime?'

'You can afford it.' He points at the bankcard. I

immediately curl my fingers around it, holding it tight against my stomach.

'Push off. Go harass someone else.'

The man-child stares at me blankly then slinks off. I blink. Beggars aren't very tough in Shyness. I was prepared to go at least another two rounds with him.

'Seven-fifty.'

Beer sloshes against my back and I turn to face the bar. The barman has his hand out for payment. I slip him the card. He looks down at it, flips it over.

'No name.'

'It's a company card.' That's what Neil says when he shouts us lunch. I'm good at thinking on my feet.

The barman nods, satisfied. The machine whirrs and prints a receipt. It wasn't a fluke in the black market; the card really does work.

'Here you are, miss.'

The barman is acting strangely; his arrogance has been replaced with grudging respect. All for a stupid credit card that's not even mine. I sign the receipt, wedge the card deep in the pocket of my hotpants and grab the drinks. The barman has placed the glasses on cardboard coasters emblazoned with the name of the club: Little Death. I take one as a souvenir.

The DJ changes tunes to something heavier as I cross the floor, trying not to spill the drinks. The bass thrums in my throat and pounds my chest. Wolfboy's teeth shine as I push through the crowd to him. His smiling eyes settle on my face. His two friends stare as I hand him the beer. Wolfboy drapes his arm casually across my shoulders. I wonder what he's told them about me. I guess it's a good sign that he's not ashamed to be seen with his arm around me in public.

'Wildgirl, this is Thom.' He points to the guy in a military-style jacket, and then to the shorter guy, who looks even younger than me. 'And Paul. We all went to school together. And they're in the band.'

I shake hands with them both. Thom's grip is as hard as Paul's is limp.

'So is this more like it?' Wolfboy asks me.

'Yeah,' I say. 'Much better than the last place.'

'Man, I don't know why you like going to the Wing.' Paul's voice is so high it's difficult not to laugh.

'What can I say? I like slumming it.'

'You missed out the other night. At the Feldspar gig. Rick Markov was there. Thom talked to him.'

'He's not interested in amateurs like us.' Wolfboy drains half his beer in one hit. His fingers drum my shoulder. There are two girls standing close to the dancefloor. One of them is definitely looking at Wolfboy and whispering in her friend's ear. The people in here are closer to my age, but they're still all dressed in black. It's stupid I'm so worried about fitting in. I like looking different from all the clones at Southside, so I should just stick my chin up and wear my pink top with pride. The goth look doesn't suit me anyway.

'So where'd he find you?' Thom turns to me. I've already decided I don't like him. He's got a fat, wet mouth that makes everything he says sound dirty. And he's pushing his chest out so I can admire his t-shirt, which is printed with the name of some band I've never heard of.

'Don't you mean where did *I* find *him*?' I wish I could plunge onto the tangled dancefloor, where people won't look at me. But Thom won't let go that easily. For a split second I panic that he's seen the photo. But that's not possible.

'You from the City?' Thom asks, before forgetting me in an instant. 'Jeth, he's here. Rick Markov!'

We all look to where Thom is pointing. I can't see a thing but the others seem to see exactly who he means.

'I told him about this place and he said he'd come, but, like, I didn't think he actually would.'

Thom's carefully maintained cool falls away as if it was never there.

'Go over, Jeth. He wants to meet you.'

'Nah, man. I'm gonna stay here and hang out.' Wolfboy nods quickly in my direction. He thinks I don't see it, but believe me, I notice *everything*. The nod makes me feel better; he was so upset after the Kidds mugged us I thought he was close to sending me home.

'You hang out with us every day. I've got nothing left to say to you, bro.'

'Well, I've got nothing to say to Rick Markov.'

'You gonna give up this opportunity 'cause one hot chick pays you a bit of attention?'

Wolfboy's eyes don't leave mine as Thom drags him away. *Sorry* and *I promise*, they seem to say, but that could just be wishful thinking. Wolfboy's taller and broader than Thom and could take him easily in a fight, but it's obvious who's the boss in this little trio. I know who Thom is. He's the guy who's popular because he's good at some random thing deemed worthy, like rugby or guitar, but who mostly stays popular because he's a minor-league bully.

Thom and Wolfboy sit down on the other side of the room, at a booth crowded with people. Paul and I are left alone, standing by the wall. I look around the crowded club, feeling abandoned. I've only known Wolfboy for, what? a couple of hours at the most, but already he's my lifebuoy in this strange place. That's not right. I've got to toughen up. I can have an adventure on my own in this big, crazy club. Wolfboy's already done more than enough to help me forget my problems.

'Producer,' mumbles Paul, looking into his glass. 'A big-deal music producer.'

There's a pause. I drain my soda water and put the glass on the ground, shift my bag to my other shoulder and look at my feet. Paul doesn't seem too thrilled to be left alone with me, but maybe he's just pissed that his friends ditched him to go talk to someone important.

India was just a story for Wolfboy, the first country that came to mind. I've already got myself a passport, ready for the moment I finish school and finally save enough money to get away. Anywhere, so long as it's not Plexus. I can take the names they call me, and the signs they put on my locker, and I can handle sitting alone to eat lunch, but this? This is not something I know how to deal with. I got through the day, but I'm never going back there again.

I told Lupe everything. I didn't mean to, but as soon as we were alone I suddenly wanted to.

It was hard to explain.

Lupe had no idea how email worked, or Photoshop. I had to explain how some girls from school had put together a photo of me with this guy I'd never seen before in my life. That they made it look like the photographer had caught me in the act; I was turning towards the camera with my top undone and my shirt hitched up around my waist. And how you couldn't even see the join; you couldn't tell they'd stuck my head on someone else's body. Even I thought it looked real.

And then they'd emailed the photo to the whole year level. And not just that; there were other names in the address field that I didn't even recognise: boys, girls, other years, other schools. It's too juicy not to forward. By now hundreds of people have probably seen it. Maybe more. There's no way I can tell every single person that the girl in the photo isn't really me.

I felt ashamed telling the story to Lupe, as if I'd actually done something wrong. I told her about everything except the card and my plan to escape. I didn't want her to say the sorts of things adults say. Like: Won't your mum be worried sick when you leave her? What will you do when the money runs out?

'So, uh…do you come here often?'

I have to blink several times to bring myself back into the noisy room. Paul is looking at me. I'm not sure if it's because I'm a girl, or not from around here, but all his earlier vivacity has fled. His brown eyes are anxious behind his round glasses.

'Nup. It's cool, I like it.'

'Little Death is all right. Umbra isn't bad either, but for some reason this is always where we end up.'

Just when I thought living in Shyness meant always being scared or depressed or living in fear of monkey-muggings, here's a room full of people enjoying themselves. And the best thing is no one here knows me at all.

'Is this place always open? I mean, if it's always night then how do you know when to go out?'

'It never really closes. But there are quiet and busy times. People seem to know. I mean, there's a rhythm to Shyness, but it takes a while to feel it.'

'I don't think I'm feeling it yet.' The only rhythm I can feel is the pulsing music soaking into my skin, spreading to my fingers and toes. I'm going to need to dance soon. Paul has the most incredible shoes on: black patent loafers fastened with buckles in the shape of bats. They're at odds with his shabby jeans and inside-out t-shirt.

'It's nice to see Wolfboy out with a girl.' Paul looks over to where Thom and Wolfboy are still sitting with the record guy.

'What do you mean?'

Two pink circles bloom on Paul's cheeks. He's just realised he's supposed to make Wolfboy sound like a stud.

'He's having fun, I can tell. Sometimes I think he doesn't ever want to feel good, not after his brother died. It's like he's trying to punish himself by not letting himself ever be happy.'

His brother.

Ortolan used to go out with Wolfboy's brother.

And now he's dead.

More people have poured into the club and I can't see Wolfboy anymore. I feel sick and sad thinking about him losing someone close to him. The strange vibe at the Raven's Wing makes more sense now: why Ortolan was so sad, and Wolfboy so uncomfortable.

'Of course,' I say. And then I'm silent. It's a trick I learnt from the shrink. To make people talk you have to be a blank white wall that they want to paint their stories on. No judgments, no reactions and no curiosity.

Paul leans against the wall at an uncomfortable angle. His glass is empty so I figure he might be in a talkative mood.

'Gram was like a god to us all,' Paul continues. 'He was, you know, good-looking, fucking lovely, got along with anyone. Him and Ortie, they were the best couple. Even before I liked girls I used to look at those two and think, I want that. One day, that's what I want.'

'I guess that makes it extra sad, what happened.' I feel my way as I go.

'He never got over it,' says Paul, pushing his floppy hair back. He looks like he has a bad case of sunburn. 'I don't know why I brought this up. I'm drunk.'

I'm desperate to hear more, but I don't want to push it. Paul's kind of wasted, and Shyness is dragging everyone down again.

'Your face has gone all red,' I tell Paul.

'It's an Asian thing. It always happens when I drink.'

I squint, but for the life of me I can't see what the hell

Wolfboy's doing over in that booth. I feel a rush of gratitude towards Paul for giving me a few more pieces of the Wolfboy puzzle. The music is louder and faster than ever, thumping against the stone walls. The kind of music you can lose yourself in. Paul and I can have fun on our own for a little while.

'Let's go dance,' I say, grabbing him by the elbow.

thirteen

I realise that my lighter is missing while I'm sitting with Thom and Rick Markov and all of Markov's many girlfriends. I play with the lighter a lot. It's a comfort thing, the way other people bite their nails or crack their knuckles. Sometimes I flick the top open and closed; other times I let it sit in my palm, anchoring me.

I pat the pockets of my jeans one more time. Empty, except for my wallet and keys. My shirt pocket houses my phone, nothing else. Thom drones on beside me, talking about our (his) influences and our non-existent musical philosophy. Rick Markov appears to be barely awake, let alone listening. The whole time Thom talks, Markov strokes the leg of the woman next to him.

I can't sit here anymore. I stand up, avoiding Thom's eyes, and shuffle out of the booth. Someone slaps me on the arse as I go and a woman cackles.

I had the lighter when I was at the black market. After I used it I put it back in my pocket, as usual. And then we met the Kidds. It's not difficult to work out what happened. It was probably the boy and girl who were behind me. They could have been playing stoned so that we didn't take them seriously. It's been done before. You should never let the Kidds out of your sight while they're rolling. I was too busy worrying about Wildgirl's safety to remember the basic rules.

I seek out the darkest part of the room, close to where the wire fence stops people falling into the disused subway tunnel. I slip around the corner and through a gap where the fence doesn't quite meet the wall. A shadowy couple are all over each other at the end of the narrow platform. I ignore them and sit on a concrete block overlooking the abyss.

Ortolan gave the lighter to Gram on his eighteenth birthday and it has their initials engraved on the base in tiny letters that no one ever notices. That lighter is the only piece of Gram I have left. Soon after he died Mum cleared all of his stuff out of the garage. She donated some to charity and threw the rest out. I suppose she also went over to Gram's flat and did the same thing. She kept just a handful of photos, and the lighter, which she gave to me when my dad wasn't around. It was a strange thing for her to do because she's so anti-smoking.

There isn't a single light in the tunnel. Occasionally a gust of cold air passes through. I'm pretty sure the couple has started removing bits of clothing but I can't find it in me to be embarrassed. I should be burning mad, I should be doing something, swearing revenge or murder on the Kidds who stole my lighter, but I'm dead inside. I feel so heavy it wouldn't surprise me if I never moved from this place, if I turned into concrete myself.

I don't know how long I'm sitting there before I wonder if Wildgirl is all right on her own. I force myself to stand up and go back into the main room. Wildgirl isn't near the entrance where I last saw her with Paul. I walk around the edges of the club, a sour taste in my mouth. I shouldn't have let Thom drag me away. She's probably furious.

I finally spot her on the dancefloor, in the centre of the sunken pit of bodies. She dances with every part of herself, her eyes closed, her hair leaping as she twists and jumps and spins. She leaves everyone else in the shade.

Paul jumps next to her in his usual twitchy way, occasionally bashing out a bit of air drum, his hair plastered across his face. They're both grinning and windmilling their arms. It looks like I shouldn't have worried.

I hang back and watch, hidden in a forest of people. You can tell Wildgirl isn't dancing for the people around her. The music moves through her body like electricity. My sickness eases a bit as I watch her. She's one good thing in my night.

After a minute I slide up behind her, putting my face close to her warm neck. She smells of vanilla and beer. For a second I think I'm going to lick her, from the curve of her neck up to her ear.

'Sorry,' I say in her ear instead. Sorry for letting Thom drag me away, and yes, sorry for thinking about licking her face.

Wildgirl whirls around, but she doesn't stop dancing and she doesn't back away. Instead she holds my shoulders and shakes it in front of me. She looks happy to see me.

'You gotta stop apologising!' she yells. Her forehead is damp with sweat.

I'm not much for dancing, at least not until I've had a drink or ten. But thinking about dancing is better than thinking about the lighter. I move closer to Wildgirl, trying to match my movement to hers, trying to feel the beat, praying my feet will somehow do the right thing. Sometimes when I'm playing guitar everything falls away and I play without thinking about what my fingers are doing. I know that's the trick to dancing as well, but I can't ever get to that place.

Paul notes me on the dancefloor with surprise and then turns his back on us, always the tactful one.

'I'm sorry I left you alone.'

'No problem. Paul is cool. We had a nice chat.'

That's the first time I've heard the words 'Paul' and 'cool' used in the same sentence.

'What did you two talk about?'

'Oh, nothing much. He was just carrying on about how The Long Blinks are the best band ever and how you're going to take over the world.'

Taking over the world sounds more like Thom's spin, but it's true that Paul and Thom both see more of a future in the band than I do. If I had to choose which of my friends to leave Wildgirl alone with then Paul's the obvious choice. Thom can be a nightmare, the way he has to impress everyone who crosses his path. He gets worse the more he's had to drink. There's no doubt he was trying to look down Wildgirl's top earlier.

'You wanna know the truth?' I put my hand on the back of her neck, resting my fingers against the bumps of her spine. 'We suck. I can't sing in tune, Paul can't keep time, and Thom can barely play three notes. We're not taking over anything. It's something we do to make time pass.'

'You're smiling about it, though.' Wildgirl looks at me from under her snake-green lids. You'd think that confessing how hopeless I am to the girl I'm desperate to impress would make me want to go home and bang my head against the wall, but instead I feel relief. A hot-and-cold rush goes through me.

I howl.

I howl at the roof like a hotted-up bomb doing donuts, full of screeches. I howl like an air-raid siren, my arms stretched out wide. Howls are like songs. They can't be summoned; they just happen. They come from a place that I barely understand. And then something else climbs to the surface, something black and jagged, something from the deep. Imagine all your worst feelings surfacing. Imagine coughing up razor blades. Imagine not being able to stop the pain from coming out, and not knowing when it's going to end.

Wildgirl laughs and whoops at the ceiling. She doesn't hear the razor blades. All around us people are laughing and clapping and punching the air. My throat burns. It always feels like this: pain and relief at the same time.

I pull Wildgirl into me to cover the shakiness I suddenly feel, and the fact that I might cry.

'This is why you don't leave, isn't it?'

'What is?'

'This! Little Death, the people here, it's cool. I can see why you don't leave Shyness, go and live somewhere else.'

'I crossed into Panwood during the day last summer.'

I don't want her to look at me so I keep my mouth by her ear. 'And I thought I was going to melt, the light was so bright.'

The real reasons why I don't leave Shyness, why I'm stuck here, why I can't leave, are so many I wouldn't know where to start. Do I even know myself? I rest my cheek against Wildgirl's hair, and then, over her shoulder, I see something that makes me bite down so hard I taste blood on my lip.

The Elf stands on the other side of the dancefloor, his eyes cutting a direct path through the crowd. I stare back for several seconds before I accept that he's really here. What more does he want from me? I look up at the ceiling and down by our feet. Someone once told me that Little Death has an electric roof to stop the tarsier from coming down here, but it doesn't hurt to check. There aren't any other Kidds on the dancefloor, but I pull Wildgirl away regardless. Every instinct tells me to put some space between the Elf and me. Don't think. Just move.

'What's wrong?'

'Kidds,' I tell her. Her eyebrows shoot up. She tries to see over the crowd.

'Where? Are they the same ones?'

I keep her moving. 'It's the Elf.'

'How did he get in here? Isn't he too young?'

'There's probably a back way. Come on, let's go.'

Thom is talking to a girl on the fringe of the pit but I drop my head and keep moving. Rick Markov is still sitting at the booth, surrounded by his posse and a table full of empties. On this side of the room there's a short tunnel with rooms leading off both sides. I glance back to see if the Elf is following, but his blond hair is still visible on the dancefloor. Has he been tailing us all this time, or did someone tip him off?

We turn left at the end of the tunnel. At the next door I brush aside the curtain to let Wildgirl through. A wisp of smoke escapes.

'Welcome to Dreamland. No one will bother us here.'

The smoke machine is turned on high and lasers swoop through the mist. Even with my enhanced eyesight it's hard to see straight. A place of illusions, just the way Dreamers like it, and a good place to hide. There's a band in here somewhere, playing low, tripped-out jams with swirling guitar. Dreamer-rock isn't loud enough or angry enough for me, but I don't mind listening to it sometimes. I lead Wildgirl across the room.

There's a free couch in the mist, tucked next to a pillar. We sit and Wildgirl watches everyone with an entranced look on her face. I've noticed she has this ability to soak up everything around her like nothing else exists.

A guy sitting on the floor near us can't stop his chin sinking to his chest, and his girlfriend has already gone foetal next to him. Beyond them, a group dance, straight-armed and straight-legged, like a film being played at the wrong speed. Behind the dancers there's the silver glint of a drum kit, and a bar in the far corner. The barman leans against the wall, arms crossed, bored out of his brain. Dreamers don't drink much.

'Land of Nod,' Wildgirl whispers.

'Little Death is different. You get everyone here—dreamers, ghostniks, necroheads—everyone. It's not segregated like other places.'

Wildgirl relaxes into the couch. I slump as well, looking back at her. I force my fists to unclench. Our faces are only centimetres apart. Everything stops around us, and it's us two, alone in the room, cocooned by the smoke.

'Even your sort?'

My sort.

'Not really. I've seen a few people in Shyness who look like me, but they're all less…changed than I am.'

Wildgirl traps my hand between hers. She pushes her fingers through the thick hair on the back of my hand.

'When I first saw you,' she says, 'I knew you wouldn't be like anyone I've ever met.'

'I didn't choose this. Not like the Dreamers. They've chosen who they are.'

And they could return to who they used to be if they

wanted to. I don't think there's any way I can go back from here.

'I look the way I do. And I act differently, without knowing why. I howl and my senses are sharper than ever. I'm never cold and I can open beer bottles with my teeth.' That last one really impresses Thom. He often wheels me out at parties to show people.

'When did it happen?'

'Slowly. Like the Darkness.'

I don't feel different on the inside. Or if I do it's hard to tell—everything is so complicated around here that I have no idea who I would be in a normal place with normal people.

'You haven't told me everything yet. Not nearly.'

Wildgirl looks amazing in this light, bronzed and otherworldly.

'It would take all night,' I say.

'We have all night.'

I can't argue with that. For some reason I find it easier to talk to Wildgirl than other people. I look down at our hands. I'm finally getting the idea that she's interested in me more than Shyness. She's more than I deserve.

'You do look different. You *are* different.' Wildgirl speaks as if she's thinking her ideas through as she's going. 'I think we like the attention our looks get us. But we also hate it.'

Maybe. Looking different sets me apart and that's both good and bad. Good for getting free drinks. Bad for feeling like anyone understands what I'm going through.

'I want people to look at me,' she continues. 'I mean, I dress in a way that makes them look at me, but then when they *actually* do, I hate them for it. Is that crazy?'

A little bit. 'Does that mean you hate me?'

'Huh?'

'Because I've been looking at you for hours.'

She laughs then, and gives me a playful slap on the arm. The imprint of her fingers burns before fading.

'I think it's fine to use your looks, but you have to have other things you can rely on as well. My mum still doesn't think anyone would be interested in her for any other reason. And—'

The irony is, I'm looking at Wildgirl and all I want to do is touch her soft cheeks and raven hair.

'—and so that's why I've decided to get my forklift licence.'

The look on my face must be priceless because Wildgirl laughs and slaps her thighs. I find myself laughing as well. I wonder if they put something in the smoke here because I'm half gone. Wildgirl taps my arm.

'Did you tell Thom and Paul?'

'Tell them what?'

'That I'm joining the band with my awesome rock-ukulele licks?'

I can't believe how funny she is. I've hit the jackpot here. If I was a different person, if my life was less complicated, if I had more to offer her than just sadness, if I didn't feel so tired from the weight of the entire world pressing down on me, then this would be the moment I would try to kiss her.

14

I'm pretty sure we're having a
moment, when Wolfboy pulls right away from me, sits up
straight and asks, 'Do you want another drink?'

I try not to look disappointed. Clearly my radar is not
operating properly with all the Dreamer smoke and the
waa-waa music. I could have sworn one of us was about
to lean in that extra few centimetres. 'Sure.' I dig into my
pocket for the gold card. 'Let's abuse the plastic again.'

'What do you want?'

Even in this light the card gleams with promise. I'm
going to cover so many kilometres with the help of this
baby. 'Whatever you're having. I still can't believe they
didn't find this. We got off so lightly.'

Wolfboy frowns. 'Not so lightly.'

'What do you mean?'

Wolfboy shrugs and stares at the Dreamers marching on the spot. Someone really needs to teach these people how to loosen up.

'They took my lighter. Got into my pocket without me noticing.'

'That's crazy. They didn't go anywhere near you.'

At least I don't think they did. The attack is a blur now. Anything could have happened while that tarsier was groping me. I remember Wolfboy helping Sebastien light his stupid candelabra at the bowling alley. He had a lighter then.

'Did you leave it at the black market?'

'No. I definitely had it in my pocket when the Kidds rolled us. And now I don't.'

He seems annoyed, but he hasn't had a cigarette all night, at least not in front of me. It already seems impossible that I was making him laugh a minute ago. Maybe I'm being too funny. Maybe he thinks I'm a clown. Clowns aren't sexy.

'A nice lighter or a crappy one?'

'A nice one. Silver. Engraved.'

'Did they take anything else?'

'No. That was it.'

At least they didn't get his wallet or phone.

'I haven't seen you smoke at all tonight.'

'I don't smoke.'

'Why do you have a lighter then?'

'I don't know. It's just something I carry around. It's my brother's.'

I sit upright, and slap him on the knee repeatedly until he turns around to face me.

'And you're only telling me this now? Why did we walk away from the Elf? Let's go ask for it back!'

'Chill out. It's just a lighter.'

Wolfboy *might* have convinced me that he doesn't care, if I didn't know about his brother, and if I didn't see that his eyes are flat and dead now when he speaks.

'It's NOT—' I have to be careful here. I'm not supposed to know about Gram, and what Wolfboy really meant when he said *not so lightly*. 'It's not just a lighter; it's the principle of it.'

'You sound like my dad.'

'I think we should try to get it back.'

'We don't even know for sure it's the Kidds.' Wolfboy avoids my eyes. He knows as well as I do who's responsible.

'Yes, we do. And what's more, we know which ones. Aren't you furious?'

I give up on staying calm. I hope Wolfboy knows that I'm not angry at him. But I can tell by the way he scowls that he doesn't know this, not really.

'We're going after them.'

'No way.'

I have to make him see things my way, but I realise that I've got more chance of convincing him if I go easy. I force my voice down. 'You can't let people walk all over you; sometimes you've got to fight back.'

'It's just a lighter,' he says again.

Yeah, it's just a lighter, like, oh, that was just a photo. But I let him have that one. If he doesn't want to tell me about Gram then I won't force him. But it's my duty to stop him from being a doormat. I can see him shutting down right in front of my eyes, locking doors and pulling across curtains to keep me out of his business, but I won't let him.

'Let's not live like we're scared. It's such a waste to be scared.'

'You don't know what you're getting into.'

'I'm going after them with or without you, so make up your mind.'

I pick up my bag and ukulele and push myself off the couch. But I've lost the exit in the dreamy mist and I take only a few confused steps before I stop. He might not want to kiss me, but I know for sure he doesn't want me wandering around Shyness on my own.

'Wait.'

His hand is on my shoulder. He doesn't see the smile

spread across my face. I don't know what I would have done if he hadn't followed me. When I have my face under control I turn around. Wolfboy looks genuinely worried, in a way that I don't understand. I can't believe he's that scared of the Kidds.

'We'll live to regret this, you know that?' he says.

He's wrong. What I'd regret is not taking back a little control. I drag him out of the Land of Nod before he has a chance to change his mind.

Little Death is even more crowded than earlier. We fight against the tide of bodies in the narrow tunnel. I clutch Wolfboy's hand, trying to keep close, but he only grips my fingers for a few seconds before letting them go. He takes us to the steps in front of the bar and we look out onto the dancefloor. The Elf's fake blond head isn't among the dancers. We check every dark corner of every room in the club. Paul is gone. Thom is gone. Rick Markov is gone. And the Elf is nowhere to be seen.

Wolfboy's house is a two-storey cream building in what clearly used to be a nice area. The houses are all sprawling mansions on large blocks, their former luxury still visible through disrepair and grime. Double garages. Satellite dishes. Lap pools. I was expecting a warehouse squat, or a depressing bedsit, or maybe even just a sleeping bag under a bridge. Those ideas seem stupid now.

Wolfboy looks out of place on his own doorstep as he fumbles with his keys and waves me stiffly into the house. I feel a tickle of apprehension deep in my stomach as I squeeze past him. My mother always told me not to go back to a wolf's lair. Oh hang on, that was a strange man's house, wasn't it? Either way, I'm pretty sure she wouldn't approve.

The ground floor of the house is dark and quiet and empty. A long hallway runs through the middle, with rooms leading off either side. Wolfboy shows me in to the front room and lights an old-fashioned kerosene lamp. The room is spacious, with polished floorboards, lemon walls and heavy velvet curtains. Sheets are draped over some furniture in the far corner, and there are faded rectangles on the walls where paintings or photos must have once hung. Everything is deathly still; even the dust motes seem to hang in midair.

'I'll get us something to drink.' Wolfboy dawdles at the doorway as if he has more to add, but then he leaves. I look around the room, trawling for details. There's not much to go on. No knick-knacks on the mantelpiece, no magazines on the coffee table, no cushions on the couch, but it's still obvious this used to be a family home.

I can hear Wolfboy opening and closing cupboards in what must be the kitchen, towards the rear of the house. He's talking to himself, or singing.

I circle the room, brushing my hands over the couch, and the smooth walls and the curtains, until I come to the ghost furniture. I lift one dusty corner of a sheet. There's a fancy cabinet underneath, made of polished wood with glass doors and brass handles. It's beautiful. I'd love to have things like this around me every day. Our furniture is St Vinnies all the way. On the top of the cabinet there's a crystal bowl full of shrivelled-up flowers, a pair of silver tongs, and a photo frame turned facedown.

I pick up the photo and bring it into the poor light. Three people pose under a large tree—a couple in their early fifties, leaning into each other, and, standing apart from them, a guy in his mid teens with crossed arms. At first I think it's Wolfboy—a younger, cleaner-cut version— but then I see a fourth person, a little boy perched in the tree. *That's* Wolfboy: freckly and impish and thoroughly adorable. The teenager is Gram. It was an easy mistake though; when I look closely at Gram there are shades of Wolfboy in his eyes, and in the tense way he holds himself. It's obvious now the photo is old: Wolfboy's mum wears a dated dress with puffy sleeves. Gram doesn't want to be there. His mum looks across at him, her expression anxious, but the older man stares straight ahead.

I hear Wolfboy in the hallway. I put the photo back, drop the sheet and race to the couch. Wolfboy brings a tray in and sits next to me. His hair has suspiciously neatened itself while he was in the kitchen. I wipe my dusty fingers clean on the couch.

'I don't know how you take it.' Wolfboy pours thick brown liquid into miniature coffee cups. 'I'm hoping it's black, because I don't have any milk or sugar.'

I take a sip and pull a shocked face, which should have made Wolfboy smile but doesn't.

'Turkish,' he says.

I keep drinking despite the bitterness—it's hot and it'll keep me awake until sunrise. Or the time when the sun is supposed to rise.

I look around the room again. I can't stop thinking about how nice this street is, and how all the houses must have tennis courts and flat-screen TVs and god knows what else, and how, even empty, this house smacks of money and privilege.

'Is it just you living here?'

'Yeah.'

'What's upstairs?'

'Stuff.'

'Stuff?' I pull a face. 'You want to elaborate on that?'

'My bedroom.'

He's being almost as monosyllabic as he was with Ortolan.

I finish my coffee and pour myself another. I sit back into the couch and stare at him. He's annoyed with me but

I'm not going to call him on it. He can speak for himself. The pointed staring works because Wolfboy eventually leans forward.

'Do you really want to do this?'

'What's the worst that can happen?' I say.

Wolfboy just snorts and drinks his coffee. He really does look like Gram, especially around the eyes.

'Look, it's easy. We find them and we ask for your lighter back. If they refuse, we fight them for it. Or we ambush them, grab the lighter before they even know what's happening.'

Listen to me. I've never been in a fight, and I barely even know what an ambush *is*. But one of us has to get fired up. Wolfboy might be a big guy now, but I get the feeling he's been letting people walk all over him for years. He shouldn't let the Kidds take away a piece of his brother so easily.

'We need a better plan than that. I've called a friend. Someone who can help us.'

'Every second that we're not out there will make it harder to find them,' I reply. At least he's talking to me again.

'I don't think so. From what I know they usually take their loot straight to Orphanville.'

'Where?'

'Orphanville. It's where the Kidds live. A big high-rise housing complex. You can see it from my bedroom window.'

I'm halfway up the hallway before he gets a chance to call out. I pretend I haven't heard him. I pass several closed doors, an empty room and a toilet. At the end of the hallway there's a kitchen and a large living area. On the right-hand side, past the kitchen, are the stairs. Wolfboy overtakes me and blocks my way.

'I don't want you messing with my stuff.'

I grab his shoulders. 'For godsake, Wolfboy, I'm not interested in your *stuff*; I just want to see Orphanland.'

'Orphan*ville*.' He sounds more than a little exasperated but he lets me past.

Upstairs is more like a loft than a full second floor. It's chock-full of amps and speakers and desks with twiddly knobs and those things you slide up and down, and the floor is a jumble of cables and power boards. A drum kit squats in one corner; a guitar is propped against a chair. On the ceiling, a thick black cable slides through an open skylight and into the night. There must be thousands of dollars' worth of gear in here.

It reeks of sweaty boys in here, the kind of smell you'd get if you boiled up twenty teenage boys for twenty hours and distilled their essence. Eau de BO. I have to step over empty beer cans and greasy paper bags and rolls of gaffer tape and scrunched-up tissues to get to the end of the room, where there's an open doorway that must lead to Wolfboy's bedroom.

The bedroom is not as bad as the band room, but it's still kind of a dump. The bed is a mattress and doona on the floor; there are clothes spilling out of garbage bags and a milk crate for a bedside table. Someone has started to paint the walls black and then given up halfway through. Tacked to the walls are hand-drawn and photocopied posters for The Long Blinks. There are wobbly stacks of books and CDs everywhere. I soak up every detail. This is where he spends his time; this is where he sleeps and dreams. These are the only ways I can find out who he is: from the things other people tell me, and from using my own two eyes.

'I didn't want you to see this.'

I immediately pretend I wasn't looking around. It doesn't smell as bad in here, probably because the window has been pushed right open.

'Don't worry; you should see my room,' I lie, and walk over to the window. The outside air is fresh against my face. Wolfboy stands next to me. He leans in close and points. 'Follow that line of trees to the right. See there? That's Orphanville.'

It's not difficult to pick out the buildings in the darkness: four black rectangles speckled with yellow lights, poking above the Shyness skyline. They remind me a bit of Plexus Commons.

'So that's where they've gone.'

'Maybe. I'm not a hundred per cent sure.'

'Why was the Elf in the club then?'

'I don't know.' Wolfboy sighs.

'Do you think he followed us to see when we noticed the lighter was missing?'

Because if that's true then they know that the lighter has sentimental value for Wolfboy, and that makes me so mad I wish that the Elf was right in front of me now so I could—words wouldn't be enough. I look at Wolfboy but he doesn't answer. I'm far angrier than he is. I bite my lip before I ask him how that could be, and look out at the towers instead.

Whenever I see my home from a distance at night I think it's so strange that each light represents one family living their life, watching telly or eating dinner or fighting, going about their business. From a distance each light is an insignificant thing, just one star in a whole galaxy.

Wolfboy's phone beeps. He's standing so close I can feel it vibrate in his shirt pocket.

'Good,' he says, checking the message. He passes a hand quickly over his hair, even though it's still perfect. 'She's here.'

15

It's difficult to say how old the girl is. Her shirt is at least three sizes too big and she refuses to meet my eyes. At a distance it would be hard to tell if she's a boy or a girl. I cringe when Wolfboy introduces me as Wildgirl. I might have been some kind of comic book character earlier, but the more Shyness throws curve balls at me, the less I'm able to keep up the act.

Her name is Blake. There's something Japanese in the way she stands with her arms clasped in front of her, each hand tucked inside the opposite sleeve. Head bowed, dishwater hair hanging straight. She's painfully thin under her oversized clothes. Either she doesn't like her body or she has to wear hand-me-downs.

I hold Wolfboy back in the hallway when Blake walks into the front room. 'How much have you told her?'

'I told her that the Kidds stole something from us and we have to get it back.'

'I don't think we should tell her about the card.'

'Why would I tell her about that? It's got nothing to do with my lighter.'

'I don't know.' He's been friends with this girl far longer than he's known me, so how am I supposed to know what kinds of things they tell each other? 'I just thought I'd check.'

Wolfboy gives me a look like I've gravely insulted his intelligence and walks into the room. Blake is sitting on the couch. Wolfboy uncovers some extra chairs and we sit around in a circle, waiting for her to say something. She twists her hands in her lap and I note her hunched shoulders, bitten-down fingernails and holey sneakers. She looks as helpless as a kitten dangling above a bucket of water.

Eventually Wolfboy figures out that Blake is not about to speak any time soon. 'Blake used to be in a gang,' he tells me. 'The Kidds. She left her unit, the Six-Sevens, five months ago and has been in hiding ever since. The leader of the Six-Sevens is the Elf.'

Wolfboy taps Blake, and she rolls up her jumper sleeves. She holds her arms out in front of her, palms up. There are thick welts on her arms, deep red valleys alternating with ridges of pale shiny scar tissue. Blake glances up at Wolfboy, but she still hasn't looked at me.

No one needs to tell me who made those marks. They're the reason why Wolfboy made me cooperate with the Kidds earlier. I force myself to look again, even though the sight makes me nauseous. This is what we're up against. No wonder she's so skittish.

'He didn't do this for discipline when Blake was still in his unit,' explains Wolfboy. I notice he doesn't look at Blake's wounds even while he's talking about them. 'He did this after she'd left the gang. Tracked her down and made sure she was punished for leaving him.'

Blake rolls her sleeves down. If someone did that to me or my mum, I would stop at nothing to pay them back. Maybe I would include Mike on the list as well if I knew where he lived now. And Nan if she was still alive. That's a pretty short list of people I'd kill for.

'What sort of bike did you ride?'

It's exactly the right question to ask. Blake finally looks at me. Her eyes are a surprising green. I wonder if she wants us to do something equally bad to the Elf when we catch up with him.

'An old Mongoose that belonged to my uncle. I've still got it, but it's not my everyday bike.'

Blake is pretty when she smiles. I haven't decided yet if she has the hots for Wolfboy.

'I used to own a Villain,' I tell her and she nods in appreciation.

'That's a good bike. But I prefer the older ones. Or putting them together myself from all different parts.'

I'm only telling half a lie. I did ride a Villain when I was younger, but it belonged to my best friend, Mike. He'd never let me ride it out of his sight. The rest of the time I had to get around on this awful pink thing with a plastic basket strapped to the front.

One of the first things I noticed when those Kidds jumped us was that their bikes were tricked out with three-spoke tuffs and bear-trap pedals. They were spending time and money on their rides. One of them even had playing cards woven between her spokes so the wheels would sing at top speed. Mike and I used to do that and pretend we were racing motorbikes.

'Six-Sevens, what does that mean?'

'It's where the unit lives, in Orphanville. Building Six, Level Seven.' Her voice is low for a girl, and it never rises or falls. I have to lean in to hear what she's saying.

'Wolfboy thinks they've taken his lighter straight to Orphanville.'

'He's probably right. The Elf collects everything and tallies it up. Then he reports to the people above him. When everyone's taken their cut, the Elf gives his unit their share.'

'Who are the people at the top?'

'I don't know. I didn't think it was worth asking. I was just happy to have a place to live.'

'The thing is, Blake, they *didn't* go straight back to Orphanville after they mugged us. We saw them after at Little Death.'

Wolfboy jumps in. 'Not all of them. We only saw the Elf. We assumed that his unit was at the club with him, but they could have already gone to Orphanville.'

'There *were* other Kidds there,' I say. I'd forgotten. 'This strange little guy tried to talk me into buying him a drink. But I'm sure he wasn't one of the Six-Sevens. I would have recognised him.'

'I don't like it,' Blake says. 'It sounds weird. If I were you, I'd leave it.'

At first glance I would have said Blake was about thirteen. Now that we're talking I realise that she's probably closer to fifteen. I can't pick anyone's age in Shyness.

'I'm not scared,' I tell Blake. That's a lie. After seeing her scars, I'm a little bit scared. But I'm still going to do it. Blake must think we're certifiable, chasing after something so small. Unless Wolfboy trusts her more than me and has already told her everything about the lighter and his brother. I wonder what else he could be holding back from me.

'Well, you should be.' Wolfboy crosses his arms. I realise

he thought talking to Blake would put me off. Not so easy, buddy.

'Well, I'm not. We're going to Orphanville.' I turn to Blake. 'You'll come with us at least part of the way, won't you?'

Wolfboy answers for her. 'No. We'll do it alone.'

They must have worked this out earlier on the phone.

Blake shrugs. 'I can't. If the Elf finds me near Orphanville he'll kill me.'

I suppose that's a good enough reason.

Blake pulls a folded-up piece of paper out of her pocket. Wolfboy drags the coffee table over and Blake lays the paper flat.

'Where do you live now?' I ask.

'There's this woman who runs a program for people who have left the Kidds. Sort of like Witness Protection,' Wolfboy says. 'Blake has to be careful who she talks to.'

'Sharon would kill me if she knew I was here.'

'What about your mum and dad? Can't they protect you?'

Blake looks up. 'Both my mums don't want anything to do with me. I did some bad things when I was with the Kidds. I lied and I stole and I did—other things.'

'You haven't called them to let them know you're out though, have you? How do you know what they want?'

Blake gives Wolfboy a look of pure irritation. They've had this conversation before.

'I *can't*,' she says, and turns back to the piece of paper. On it is a map of Orphanville, sketched in blue biro.

Orphanville is bigger than I expected. There are twelve numbered rectangles for the twelve towers of flats. I could only see a few towers from Wolfboy's window. A handful of other buildings are marked with smaller squares, and there's a dashed line around the edge of the paper: a fence.

'The best way to get there is from the river side.' Blake adds two parallel lines outside the fence. I bend my neck at an awkward angle, trying to see what she's doing.

'There's a path along the eastern bank. You go past the power station, and at the next bridge you're right behind Orphanville. You climb up a steep hill here, and find a way through the fence. Once you're there you should go to Building Six.'

Blake caps her pen and my mind races. What else do we need to know?

'How many Kidds are in the Six-Sevens?'

'Five. The Elf, Baby, Trisha, Shannon, and my replacement is a Kidd called Cassius. I don't know much about him, but watch out for Trisha 'cause she carries a knife. Shannon can fight as well, but you need to watch out most for the Elf. He can climb anything, even walls that look like there's nothing to grip on to.'

They sound superhuman to me, not like children at all. Wolfboy folds up the map and puts it in the pocket of his jeans. I get my last few questions in.

'If we wanted to bribe one of them what would we offer? What's something they want that they can't get?'

'Bribes won't work. They don't need anything from outsiders.'

'Then what matters most to them? What can we threaten them with?'

'Honestly?' says Blake. 'They're fearless. They don't care about anyone but themselves. Threats won't work. Bribes won't work. I hope you get lucky and don't even find them. But if you do run into them you'd better be ready to fight dirty.'

sixteen

We work fast, without thought. I swap my checked shirt for a black t-shirt, and find a pair of jeans, a black turtleneck and a navy beanie for Wildgirl. I pull my old bike out of the garage. It's dusty and spotted with rust but it seems sound enough. While Wildgirl pumps up the tyres, oils the chain and rips off the reflectors, I put some things from the garage into my backpack: a coil of rope, a plastic sheet, octopus straps, pliers, gaffer tape, a shifter. I grab Dad's old fishing knife and wrap it in a rag.

I feel like I'm watching myself do these things. If I don't think then I won't lose it, at anyone or anything. Wildgirl was supposed to take one look at Blake's scars and reverse at a hundred miles an hour, but she didn't even flinch.

From the kitchen I grab a packet of fun-size chocolate bars that I was given months ago for helping a friend paint his new squat. I've lost my taste for sweet things. I put the chocolate into a plastic bag then shake in a jar of Italian herbs to mask the smell.

Blake stays behind in the house—if things go badly with the Elf I don't want her on the streets—and Wildgirl takes her bike. We have to put the seat up a bit but other than that it suits her fine. Blake is already asleep on the couch when we leave, her arms folded over her head.

We ride around the driveway a few times to check the bikes and then pull out into the empty street. I haven't ridden in years. I can't remember exactly when Paul and Thom and I stopped, but it was around fifteen, when all of a sudden being seen on your bike became desperately uncool. I breathe easier now that Wildgirl isn't rattling around inside my house, touching things and asking questions, but I'm not a hundred per cent happy that we're going ahead with this. We haven't thought it through well enough.

'I feel like I'm twelve again,' Wildgirl calls out. Her handbag swings off one handlebar. She flaps her arms like a bird, riding around a roundabout until I'm dizzy. I tried to talk her into leaving her handbag behind, but she looked at me like I'd asked her to cut one of her arms off. She went through it and took out a water bottle, dog-eared book, mp3 player and sunglasses as a compromise. No amount of arguing would convince her to abandon the ukulele though, especially once she realised she could fit it inside her bag.

'Keep your voice down,' I say. It's like she's trying to draw attention to herself.

We should still be sitting in the chill-out room at Little Death with our faces nearly touching, the only two people in the world. Instead we're playing bike bandits on the backstreets. Of course I want the lighter back but things aren't as black and white as Wildgirl would have them. This isn't a simple decision. I could be putting Blake in danger, or there might be other ways to get the lighter back that don't involve breaking in to Orphanville. But we haven't stopped to think about that. Wildgirl says I shouldn't let people steamroll me, but that's exactly what she's done.

We hang a right into Oleander Crescent, a broad street with wedding-cake houses perched on withered lawns. Even though it's just around the corner the houses here are worth twice as much as mine, on account of their river views. A faint haze hangs near the ground, and the street looks like an abandoned film set. I can go for weeks without seeing another person walking the streets near my house. Wildgirl slows down. A trick of the lone streetlight makes the shadows cast by our bike wheels elongate until they look like spiders zooming in our wake.

'Who lives in these?' Wildgirl points to the mansions, breaking the silence.

'Most of them are empty.' The rich people on Oleander Crescent were some of the first to leave Shyness. Most owned other houses they could run away to: beach houses or rental properties in other suburbs.

'Why don't people move in?'

'They're protected by armed security services, or electric fences. People hope things will change one day and they can come back. It's impossible to sell them anyway. No one in their right mind would buy into this place.'

'Do Paul and Thom live near here?'

'What is this, twenty questions?' My voice is sharper than I intend.

'I don't have to know if it's a secret.'

I swerve to avoid a gaping pothole. 'I'll take you to see their house if we come out of this alive. It's worth a look.'

Wildgirl doesn't take the bait about whether we're going to live or not. For some reason it's enough for her that the Kidds did something wrong. Her eyes have an evangelical glint. I've seen the same look on godbods and social workers.

But Wildgirl gets to leave. I don't. Even if we don't get

caught tonight, there's always the chance that the Kidds will come for me later.

Oleander Crescent curves down towards the river and then flanks it all the way to the Avenue and the gates of Orphanville. I push my legs harder. The road banks steeply around the next bend—we used to race go-karts down here as kids—and I pump my brakes as I prepare to jump the gutter at the bottom of the hill. I don't warn Wildgirl. If we're gonna do this, she has to be able to keep up.

I hit the gutter harder than I intend and nearly fly off the bike, pulling on the handlebars to keep myself seated. We hurtle down a thin path between two houses. My back wheel sheers sideways on the gravel and I narrowly avoid a fence as I try to bring the speed wobbles under control.

I wait for Wildgirl at the end of the passageway, but she's been with me almost all the way. Running behind the mansions to our left and right is the dirt path that Blake suggested we take. The path goes all the way to Orphanville along the riverbank.

'Shit!' Wildgirl puts a foot on the ground to steady herself. Her shoulders are heaving. She uses the beanie to fan her face. 'I'm really unfit.'

'You ride well.' She didn't hesitate on the curb, and she knows a bit about bikes too. I wasn't expecting Blake and her to bond over them. I still feel slightly out of place on mine. The handlebars are too low and the pedals are unreasonably small. I'd be almost as quick on foot.

'We're not going to be seen, are we?' Wildgirl asks.

'Not if we do our job properly.'

'No, what I mean is, no one's going to see me wearing this, are they?'

She looks down at her outfit with distaste. I can't believe this is her main concern right before we go into enemy territory. The black turtleneck doesn't hide her off-the-chart body, but I'm not in the mood to reassure her.

'You look okay. I suppose.'

She gives me the finger. I guess I deserve it.

'So we take this path all the way?'

I haven't been down to the river since I stopped school. The riverbank used to be densely wooded, but now there's only a labyrinth of dead shrubs and trees. The moon has climbed high into the sky and shines down on the ribbon of water, making the surface look slick and glossy. The river is higher than I remember. In front of us is a wooden bridge.

'I've got a better idea. Come this way.'

My bike shudders across the uneven timber slats of the bridge. We'll take a slightly different route. My old school, St Judes, is on the other side of the river and there's an identical path on the other bank. I used to ride this way to school every day for almost five years.

The path is further away from the river's edge and unlit. I let rip. Wildgirl, for all her claims of being out of shape, manages to keep up. We cycle down into a dip, leafless twigs grasping for our arms and faces. I ride with one arm shielding me until the path climbs higher. On our right the ground drops sharply towards the river, and to our left it falls away gradually into a wide plain. The moon throws off enough light to see in all directions: the black river, the silvery plain and ahead the lights of Orphanville. I lower my head and pedal.

'Slow down,' Wildgirl calls. 'I want to look at where we're going.' She's pulled her beanie back on and she looks remarkably like a cycling pixie.

We slow right down until we barely have enough speed to keep us upright. Wildgirl gets her breath back in gulps, her attention fixed on the towers ahead. Orphanville looks solid and majestic from a distance, the towers sequined with specks of light. There's an orange flare at the top of one tower—someone must be having a bonfire.

Wildgirl rides closer and grips my handlebars. I reach for hers so that we're cycling along linked by our crossed arms.

'I thought I'd be scared by now.'

'I thought you'd be scared already too.' I'm enjoying the way her arm pushes against mine but I'm also annoyed that I'm swayed so much by her. Thom's words from Little Death come back to me. *You gonna give up this opportunity 'cause one hot chick pays you a bit of attention?*

The dead trees thicken around us once more, masking the river and the plain. Several times I think I glimpse figures standing in the bushes, schoolboys in maroon blazers, but when I look at them directly there's no one there. If anyone's getting spooked it's me. There are parts of Shyness where dreams and memories come thicker, and it must be this way close to the river. I wonder if Wildgirl feels it too. I have to keep talking.

'How come you know so much about bikes?'

'I used to be a real tomboy. Mike and I rode everywhere when we were kids. We'd go as far along the beach paths as we could, for kilometres and kilometres, on our own. We'd disappear for whole days.'

I tighten my grip on Wildgirl's handlebars. We're getting good at this tandem riding. I'm finding it hard to stay mad at a cycling pixie.

'Who's Mike?'

'He was my best friend. He lived in the apartment below us.'

'*Was* your best friend?'

'He moved away when I was twelve.'

I let my grip loosen a little. The path dips once more and our bikes gather speed. If we keep going along this path we'll reach the remains of a car dealership, some sports fields, and then see the spires of St Judes.

'Is that the bridge Blake was talking about?' Wildgirl points and our bikes wobble violently. I let go and we break apart.

A wooden bridge arches over the river to our right, between two large rocks. Someone has spray-painted faces on them. We must be directly behind Orphanville now. I peel off and skid to a halt at the foot of the bridge. There's a shower of dirt behind me as Wildgirl brakes.

The bridge is falling apart; almost every third plank of wood is missing. One safety rail has broken off completely.

'Looks like we're going to have to do this one by foot.'

I hop off my bike and lift it so the crossbar rests on my shoulder. Pieces of splintered wood litter the bank below. A layer of mist shifts on the surface of the river. The moon has disappeared behind an armada of clouds and everything is dark and still.

I stand close to the edge of the bridge where it looks sturdiest, and grasp the remaining safety rail with my free hand. Wildgirl does the same. The bridge curves steeply enough that I can't see what lies on the other side once we start crossing. We're just past the apex when three figures step out from under the bridge.

This is not good news.

Wildgirl lets go of her bike and keeps walking forward as if she's in a trance. I grab the bike before it falls to the ground. Every muscle in my body tenses, ready to act.

seventeen

They're dressed in black, white and red, that's the first thing I notice. Two girls, one boy. Around thirteen or fourteen years old, although it's hard to tell with their costumes. All three wear ruffled shirts and puffy black pants. Units often have a dress code, in the same way that Dreamers like to wear white and all necroheads are bald. I lay our bikes on the ground at the mouth of the bridge. I've got at least twenty centimetres and almost as many kilograms on each of them. If they're unarmed and not sugared up then I should be able to handle this.

Wildgirl calls out to the strangers, 'Who are you?'

The tallest girl speaks. It's obvious she's the leader

because she wears a big Napoleon hat and the other two stand behind her. Her hands are perched on her hips as she addresses us. 'Actually, fair maiden, the question is: who the hell are you, trip-trapping over my bridge?'

There's barely a beat before Wildgirl replies, 'Well, we're not goats, if that's what you're asking. There are three of you. So that makes *you* the goats, doesn't it?'

The captain's lip curls. She flicks her plaits over her shoulders. Her face is thin and alert and freckled.

'We're *trolls*, don't you know? We guard the bridge.'

'Well, you look more like *pirates* to me.'

Wildgirl is right. I may not be following the conversation at all, but the Kidds do look like pirates. The smaller girl even has an eye patch, although she's wearing it above her eye, rather than over it. Patch-girl speaks now, in a reedy voice that matches her reedy arms and wispy hair.

'No-oooh. We're trolls.'

They're all wired to the moon, Wildgirl included.

The captain steps up to Wildgirl, gets right up in her face, and to her credit Wildgirl doesn't back off one inch. They eyeball each other until somehow they reach a wordless agreement not to punch each other's lights out.

'We're freelancers,' says the captain. 'Freelance mushroom-merchants and bridge-keepers.'

I check all three pirates for weapons, but I can't see anyone packing. My muscles loosen and I rise from the slight crouch I didn't know I'd dropped into. Patch-girl carries a wicker basket covered with a tea towel.

'How much do the Kidds pay you to guard the bridge?' I ask the captain.

Patch-girl steps forward. 'We're not slaves. We work on our own.' She probably intends to sound disgusted, but her high voice makes her sound more like a little girl who's found fairies living at the bottom of her garden.

'So do we,' says Wildgirl. 'Me and Sasquatch here. We're trained ninjas. We studied with the Grand High Master for three years on an isolated mountaintop.'

She glances at me and I roll my eyes. Lunatic conversation. Yeah, that's exactly what we need right now.

The two girls look at me without interest and then return to Wildgirl. They don't question her unlikely story. They've realised Wildgirl's from outside and that makes her far more interesting than me. The pirate-boy hangs back, looking at us from under a scarf decorated with skull and crossbones. I nod at him but he's blank as anything.

Wildgirl and the captain both have their hands in their pockets now, seemingly having a friendly conversation.

Wildgirl looks at patch-girl's basket. 'What's in there?'

Patch-girl pulls the towel away. 'Midnight shrooms. You want some?'

Wildgirl shakes her head and patch-girl smooths the towel back into place.

'What are you doing at the river? Your sort never come around these parts.'

To my surprise, after all the ninja talk, Wildgirl tells the truth. 'We're going to break in to Orphanville. The Kidds stole something from us, and we're going to steal it back.'

Great. Tell the strangers our secret plan.

Patch-girl's eyes are a pair of shiny coins. 'Coooool.'

The captain isn't as easily impressed. 'Are you sure that's where you're going? Because as soon as I saw you I thought to myself, they're off to the velo for sure.'

'The velo?'

I'm as puzzled as Wildgirl is. I look to where the captain is pointing, further along the river, past St Judes.

'The bike place. The *dog* place.' She must be talking about the velodrome, but I've got no idea what it has to do with dogs. Maybe they used to race greyhounds there. I'm about to ask her exactly what she means when Wildgirl leaps in.

'Nope. Orphanville. That's where we're going.'

'What did the Kidds steal?'

'Something important.'

'Which unit?'

I answer for Wildgirl. 'The Six-Sevens.'

'The Elf?' The captain is surprised.

'He came this way not fifteen minutes ago,' patch-girl

butts in. 'All of them, heading back to base. It looked like something really exciting was going on!'

The captain shushes her and thinks for a moment, tugging on the waterfall of white material at her throat. When she finally speaks all the silliness has gone from her voice. 'You need to find their safe room. Every building has safe rooms. One room for every unit that lives there. The Kidds in each building are sworn to secrecy on the location of their rooms, but people talk.'

'How do you know about that?' I ask.

'I used to be a Kidd. But I didn't like the rules, so I left.'

The captain looks me straight in the eye. Against all better sense, I believe her. Behind her, pirate-boy has dropped to his hands and knees as if he's looking for something in the dirt.

'What's with him?'

'Cabin Boy Pete? He doesn't like talking much. Now. We gave you something. It's time for you to pay the toll.'

'Says who?'

'Says me. It's the rules. You cross the bridge, you pay the toll.'

'Sure. How much is it?'

I have some cash. You never know who you're gonna have to pay off around here. It's time to wind this up before someone else comes along and sees us. Two people dressed in black can fly under the radar if they're careful. Five people, including three flamboyantly dressed pirates—that's another matter.

'It will cost the handsome price of one kiss,' says the captain.

'No way.'

There's no chance I'm getting any closer to the captain than I already am. I'm no authority on pirates or trolls, but I'm guessing dental hygiene isn't high on their list of priorities.

'I didn't mean you, stupid.' She gives me a withering look and then turns to Wildgirl. At first I think the captain has a nervous twitch, but then I realise she's trying to flutter her eyelashes. She can't be serious.

Wildgirl steps forward without hesitation. 'That's fine. Pucker up, you piratical wench!'

'Wait,' says Cabin Boy Pete. He sits on his haunches and points at our bikes. The front wheel of mine still spins lazily. I look at him more closely. I've heard his voice before.

'No!' The captain is adamant. 'We don't ride bikes anymore, remember?'

'Sell them,' insists Pete, gnawing on his lip. I stare at his face, trying to figure out why he's familiar to me.

'To who? Kidds?' The captain spits on the ground and turns away from Pete. He falls back on all fours, moving his hand in a circular motion above the ground. It takes me a moment to realise that he's washing the decks of an imaginary ship with an imaginary scrubbing brush. Something catches in my brain. Pete. Peter. I do know this guy.

'Peter Kouros?'

Pete doesn't acknowledge me. He steps up his pretend-scrubbing efforts. Peter Kouros was in the year below me at school. Nice guy. He came top in nearly every subject but you would never hear him brag about it. Sometime after the Darkness began, while Paul and Thom and I were still going to classes, he disappeared. Paul knew him better than I did because they used to play chess together at lunchtime, and even he couldn't find out why Peter dropped out or where he went. Now I know. He joined the Kidds.

'What did he ever do to you?' I ask the captain. I can't believe that the boy grovelling in front of me is the same guy I used to go to school with. He's skin and bones.

'Cabin Boy did something bad. And now he wants to make it up to me.'

'What have you done to him?'

'What have I done?' The captain's voice rises. 'I rescued him. You should be asking what did *they* do to him.'

Wildgirl puts herself between the captain and me. 'We can't give you our bikes. We need them to get away. What else do you want?'

The captain is sulking now. 'I was joking about the kiss,' she says to Wildgirl. 'I might catch something off you anyway, something from outside. Sunstroke, or sunburn or something.'

'Well, I wasn't joking,' replies Wildgirl. As much as I want to throttle her for dragging this out she's undeniably better at diplomacy than I am. 'But stop stuffing us around. We're kind of in a rush. What do you want?'

Patch-girl pipes up. She's still looking at our fallen-down bikes. 'I want THAT. The red thing. I want that.'

We all look at Wildgirl's red handbag pinned underneath the handlebars. I look at Wildgirl. She shrugs, way too casually.

'That old thing? Sure, I mean, if you can put up with all the stains and the broken zip and the funky smell. Why not?'

Patch-girl looks pleadingly at the captain. Beside me, Wildgirl holds her breath.

The captain sighs. 'I guess we can use it to carry mushrooms.'

Patch-girl jumps up and down and claps her hands. Wildgirl lets out a lungful of air. She walks to her bike, gallows-slow, unhooks her bag from the handlebars, then comes up behind me and unzips my backpack. The straps tug at my shoulders when she tips the contents of her bag into mine. The ukulele doesn't fit so she slings it across her shoulders again. She passes the bag to the captain, who gives it to patch-girl, who hugs it to her chest. Good. Now we can finally get a move on.

'I'm sorry,' says the captain. 'But this is how we make a living.'

Wildgirl stares daggers at patch-girl. Peter Kouros is standing up now, his body half turned away from us as if he can't wait to leave. I put my hand on his shoulder. I can feel the sharp edge of his shoulder blade just under the skin.

'Peter,' I say quietly, 'do you remember me?' I bend down and try to catch his eye but he's stiff as a board. I wait a few moments and then I give up. I don't know what I'm hoping for. We can't take him with us to Orphanville anyway. I grab my bike and nod at Wildgirl.

'Sorry,' repeats the captain.

Wildgirl goes to pick up her bike, but at the last minute she darts across to the captain and kisses her hard on the mouth. Wildgirl dips her backwards and the captain's hat falls off. It's a real Hollywood moment. I look away. When I look back the captain is picking her hat up and saluting Wildgirl with a big grin on her face.

Wildgirl stalks to her bike without looking back. She wasn't joking in that booth about stealing hearts. The captain clicks her heels together. 'Snip, snap, snout, this tale is told out!' She waves her arm theatrically at her troop, and they fall in behind her.

I don't say anything until we're pushing our bikes up the steep hill that leads to Orphanville.

'Why did you do that?' I ask, like a stupid person.

'Give me a break,' Wildgirl says. 'Why do I do anything?'

She's puffing. I could put my hand on her back and help her up the steep incline, but I don't.

'You mean, why do you enjoy messing around with people's feelings?' I say.

'You know what? She just met me. I think she'll get over it. Are you jealous?'

'No. Why would I be jealous of a crazy person? Because they were crazy, you know. All of them.'

Including Peter. Who used to be one of the most normal people I know. Maybe I shouldn't have left him behind. I might be the only person from before who knows where he is. I look back down the slope, but already the riverbank is deserted.

'Well, those crazy people gave us an important piece of information that we wouldn't have otherwise, so I don't know what you're so shitty about.'

Wildgirl concentrates on getting her bike up the hill and freezing me out. I'm not sure if I should press on, or chase after Peter, or at least message Paul to let him know I saw him. In the end I keep moving forwards. At the top of the slope there's a strip of ground that's covered with a thin layer of dead, flattened grass. The chain-link fence is tall—over nine feet—but there's no barbed wire on top. We should be able to climb it. I balance my bike against the fence and look through. We're at the rear of Orphanville and there are fewer lights than if we were coming at it from the front. This is the closest I've ever been to the Kidds' headquarters, and it looks surprisingly ordinary. The first buildings are a hundred metres away. I make out something else in the distance, before the buildings, something that obscures our view of the grounds.

'There's another fence,' I say, surprised. 'Blake didn't put that on the map.'

Blake didn't mention anything about a safe room either, and I can't believe she'd forget to tell us something that important. She'd have to know about them, spending a year with the Kidds. I think of her alone in my house. I do my best to swallow my suspicion. There's no point getting paranoid. Blake is a good person.

I drop my backpack on the ground and find the map in my jeans pocket. Wildgirl lies flat on her back with her arms stretched out like she's making grass angels. The ukulele nestles into her side.

So that's it. Her official job is kissing strangers and lying around. My job apparently is making sense of all of this, and figuring out what to do next. Despite the fact this was all her idea. I sit down and unfold the map. There's only one fence marked on the map. I hope this doesn't mean there are other mistakes.

Wildgirl's voice rises from her bed. 'Look. We forgot about the moon.'

I follow her pointed finger. The moon sits high above us, smaller and further away now. Only a wisp of cloud remains. I hadn't forgotten about the moon for a second.

'It would be better for us if there's no moon. Less light to be seen by.' I turn back to the map with some effort, but Wildgirl tugs on my t-shirt. She pulls herself up and holds out her hand.

'What?' I'm trying to concentrate here. For someone who talked me into this, Wildgirl is showing a remarkable lack of interest in the details of our death-mission. She keeps her hand out until I realise she wants me to shake it.

'Pleased to meet you, Jethro,' she says, gripping my hand tightly with both of hers. 'My name is Nia.'

I stare at her, not really understanding.

'Nia,' she repeats. 'Not Wildgirl. Nia. That's my real name. N–I–A. It's Gaelic. Or Swahili. Looks like I'm either half-Irish or half-African. Maybe both. Stop me talking any time soon, won't you?'

'Why are you telling me this now?' I'm still staring. What is she playing at? 'Look, this isn't a game. If you're doing this so you have something to tell your friends about when you get home, don't. I don't need your help. I can do without the stupid lighter.'

'No, that's where you're wrong. You *do* need my help, only you can't see it.' Wildgirl's eyes flash with annoyance. 'I thought I should tell you my name before we go in there, because we have to be in this together. A team. No secrets and no bullshit.'

I should be pleased she told me her name. It means she trusts me, at least a little. But I wouldn't mind knowing what she means by team. Does she want me to be like her childhood friend, whatshisname?

'I'm doing this for you,' she says, even though she's glaring still. But I didn't ask you to, I want to say. I never asked for her help. Am I such a mess, such a charity case, that she has to step in?

I see myself for a second through her eyes. A guy too lazy and too cowardly to take action when he should. I'm not worth the effort, I feel like telling her. A phantom-punch curls my fingers again, and I wouldn't know who I'd choose to spend it on first. I'm so confused. If I sit here and keep thinking, something in my head is going to break. I get to my feet and squash the map in my pocket. The fence rises high above us.

'Come on. I'll give you a boost up.'

18

I finally feel fear taking hold, lying in the shadow of Orphanville. I should be relieved. It's about time I took this seriously. Wolfboy's on edge. I can see it in the way he's holding himself: coiled and ready to spring into action at a moment's notice. It isn't that I think the Kidds aren't dangerous; it's just that I've felt charmed up until now. I felt charmed from the moment I first saw Wolfboy. What kept me riding at full speed into the black night, with only the sound of Wolfboy's wheels for guidance and no real idea of what was ahead of me, was the feeling that magical things could happen tonight.

But this is different. This is real. The pale, sickly grass

is real under my fingertips and the fence and buildings in front of me are real and the pissed-off vibe I'm getting from Wolfboy is somehow more real than anything else. I take some deep breaths. We're over the first fence and we're lying close to the second, which is even taller and has coils of barbed wire along the top. On the other side are dark paddocks, wide seas of blackness, then the towers. Their outlines are fuzzy in this light, but I can fill in their shapes from the chequerboard of lights.

I run through everything that Blake told us.

Look for traps. Even the youngest Kidds can lay a good one.

Avoid sugar-stoned Kidds: you don't want to fight someone who isn't feeling any pain.

Don't help little Kidds who appear helpless or injured. They use the youngest ones as bait.

'Do you think Lupe's circle kept us safe from the pirates?' I'm looking for some reassurance. I'd like to think we're still protected. I raise myself up on one elbow to check out what's happening in the great beyond. I've got no idea why I'm whispering because there's no one in sight. I thought there might be guards, but, so far, nothing. Orphanville looks sleepy and still.

Wolfboy's reply is abrupt. 'They weren't pirates; they were children.'

He's still in a bad mood. I thought he'd appreciate

knowing my real name, but apparently not. I've derailed my entire evening for his benefit. I get that he doesn't want to rock the boat, and I get that these people really hurt a friend of his, but what I don't get is that he's angry at me and not the Kidds. I look back at the first fence, at the silhouettes of our bikes propped up against it. We should have laid them flat on the ground, or hidden them in some shrubs. If anyone walks past and sees them they'll know someone has jumped the fence.

'We need to offload some of this.'

'Why did you bring so much?' I ask, as Wolfboy empties the contents of his backpack onto the ground.

'I didn't know what we'd need.' He doesn't look at me. 'We were in a rush so I brought everything.'

'Don't dump my stuff. It's in the front pocket. I'm screwed without my phone or my house keys.' I paid for the handbag with my first pay cheque from the call centre. I don't want to lose anything else tonight.

The only thing I've kept on me, apart from the ukulele, is the bankcard; I've stashed it safely in my bra. I take the map off Wolfboy while he sorts through his bag, and try to sync up the drawing with what's in front of me. Maps are not my strong suit.

'Blake didn't say anything about the safe rooms, did she?' I may as well be talking to myself. I really hope she hasn't led us astray deliberately because if she has, this is about to get a whole lot more difficult. 'How long have you known her?'

Wolfboy's look is sharp. 'About six months. We met dumpster-diving. She probably forgot to mention it. You saw what Pete was like. I think the sugar binges mess with their memories.'

Six months isn't that long to know someone. Then again, neither is however many hours it's been for us. I drop the subject. We'll have to work with the information we've got.

The first building beyond the second fence is a low-lying square. Some sort of shed, by the looks of it. I swivel the map, trying in vain to find the corresponding square. Maybe Blake only drew the towers in correctly and the rest is just to give us an idea of what else we might find. We learnt to read maps in Geography last year, but I think I dozed through most of it.

Wolfboy holds up a pair of monster pliers. 'I knew I brought these for a reason. We'll cut through the fence.'

'Good. I wasn't looking forward to ripping myself open on the barbed wire.'

So far the night has been like an especially cruel boot camp. Wolfboy's barely raised a sweat. If you gave me a few hours I could probably even turn him into a half-decent dancer. But I'm stuffed. My chest aches, and my arms and legs have gone rag-doll floppy. Wolfboy's jeans are too big for me, and the cuffs keep dragging under my heels. I have to remind myself that I may not be the fastest runner, but I have other skills. We could have easily gotten into a fight with the pirates; instead, they were practically eating out of our hands by the end. If only I could have managed to do that with the girls at school, but things with them went wrong from the start.

'That's it.'

Wolfboy wraps the unwanted gear in a blue plastic sheet and stashes it close to the fence. 'We can pick this up on the way out.'

I'm glad he thinks that will happen. The way he's been talking you'd think we'd booked a one-way ticket to Orphanland.

'You start on the fence. I'll pack your bag.'

Wolfboy nods and begins cutting through the wire. I watch him for a few moments, staring at his hunched shoulders. He's as distant as the stars above us. It's like I imagined the closeness we had in the Dreamer room at Little Death.

I turn to the bag. There's still a lot to pack, even after the cull: a heavy length of rope, a spanner, a roll of tape. I find a knife and add it to the reject pile while Wolfboy isn't looking. Mike told me to never carry a weapon around the Commons because it could just as easily be used against me. That's a pretty weird thing for a twelve-year-old to say. Now that I think about it, those words must have come from his father: a scary ex-Army guy who never did anything but grunt at me, even though I was over at their place almost every day.

For some reason Wolfboy has packed a plastic bag full of green leaves. I put my face close to it and smell. Herbs of some sort, oregano maybe, or thyme. I hold the plastic bag out.

'Are you selling pot to the kiddies on the side?'

In the darkness the pliers look like a natural extension of Wolfboy's arm, as if he has pincers instead of hands. It's too dark to see his eyes properly. He doesn't reply so I put on my best narc voice. Mum really likes police procedural TV shows, so I do a pretty good job of it.

'So you think it's all right to peddle drugs to five-year-olds, scumbag?'

Wolfboy replies lazily, 'They're at least seven and you know it.'

I have to search for his smile in the darkness, which makes it all the better when I do find it. I convince myself that one smile means everything is all right between us. He wasn't the world's chattiest guy to begin with, and we're probably both nervous as hell. We'll be safe in there as long as we stick together.

I put the mystery herbs in the backpack.

Once we're in the grounds of Orphanville there might

not be any time to talk, and there's a few things I have to know before we cross this final fence.

'What else do you know about the Kidds?'

'Not much more than what Blake told us.'

'But you've lived like this for three years. You must know more.'

'The Kidds haven't been around that long. They only started getting organised about two years ago.'

'Did they do something to your family? Is that why your parents left?'

It's only once the words are out of my mouth that I realise I could be skating way too close to the Gram issue. Maybe the Kidds had something to do with his death. Wolfboy stops snipping the fence for a moment but doesn't look at me.

'My family left—well, they left for lots of reasons. They said it was because all their friends were leaving, and businesses were shutting down, and property values were diving. But it wasn't that. Do you know how places can turn bad? Like the things that happen there get so tangled up with the place itself, that you can't...' Wolfboy trails off, as if he's not quite saying what he means.

'I know what you mean.' I knot my fingers together and try hard not to interrupt. Finally, he's talking again. I do know what he means. They don't have to be places with bad memories. Mike and I used to hide in this shed on the rooftop of our building. We turned it into a clubhouse, even though we didn't actually have a club. But it was the place where we'd tell our secrets and smoke. Or Mike would smoke and I'd watch because I hated the taste. Mike's secrets were always bigger than mine. Since Mike moved away, I don't go there anymore. I can't even go onto the roof without feeling a tightness in my chest.

I haven't thought about Mike for years, so it's strange that I've thought about him twice in one hour. He left Plexus one day without leaving a phone number or a new address. When you're twelve there's not much you can do to track someone down. At the time I thought I'd never forgive him for abandoning me. But now I find myself wondering what happened to him. Would we become friends again if we ran into each other in the street?

Wolfboy has gone so quiet I figure that's the end of our conversation. Still, it was a start. He's almost finished cutting a flap in the wire. His hair gathers in dark curls against the pale skin of his neck. A breeze hisses over us and the pliers go snip, snip, snip. I look up and the moon is there, full and round like a big eye.

When Wolfboy's voice creeps into the moment it's barely a whisper above the rustling grass.

'If you want to know the truth, something bad did happen to my family, but it was nothing to do with the

Darkness. My brother. Gram. He was five years older than me. About four years ago, he killed himself.'

Wolfboy has stopped working on the fence, but he's still facing it, kneeling in a position of utter defeat. This is the truth that I've wanted him to tell, but now that I've heard it I wish I hadn't.

'Things had been bad for a while. With my family, with Gram. He hadn't spoken to my dad in years and he only spoke to my mum on the phone every couple of months. He didn't see eye to eye with them on anything. He broke up with his girlfriend and she moved away, overseas. They'd been together since they were sixteen and no one knew what they'd fought about, why she'd left.'

Wolfboy turns towards me. There are no tears in his eyes; they look dark and bottomless and empty.

The first question I want to ask is: how did he do it? That's always the first thing people want to know, but it's also the stupidest. I stop the words before they escape my mouth. 'It's Gram's lighter, isn't it?' I ask instead, and Wolfboy nods.

'Gram took the breakup hard. He wasn't doing well. We knew he was drinking too much and kept to himself. He was angry all the time. But no one saw it coming. Things were bad, but they didn't seem that bad.'

It doesn't sound like the end of the story, but Wolfboy looks spent. This is where I say something comforting, or wise, or even acknowledge how fucked up the whole thing is. But what can I say? I just sit there with him, the breeze fussing around us. I hope he feels my sympathy, even though I don't touch him or say anything. I feel unbearably sad. Now I understand why he was holding the full story back.

Wolfboy chose to live among the memories of his brother, and his parents chose to run away from them. I doubt they've left them behind, though. You could travel halfway across the world and the pain would still be inside you.

After a while Wolfboy reaches forward and pushes the flap of wire upwards, using both hands to bend it as high as it will go.

'It's done,' he says.

nineteen

Beyond the second fence there's fifty metres of open ground to cover before the first building. I crawl commando-style, my bag an unwelcome bulge on my back. Wildgirl lags behind. I pause for a second to make sure she's following me. She creeps forward, but rolls her eyes, letting me know she's not happy with the situation. The ukulele keeps slipping around to her front, and she keeps pushing it back irritably.

My feet drag. I feel disconnected from the task ahead of me. I want to kick myself for all the things I've told her. Adults always say: get it off your chest. Talk about it. You'll feel much better afterwards. But in my experience that's not true. I feel heavier than ever.

It takes a few minutes to reach cover. Blake warned us about booby traps, so every time I move forward I examine the dirt ahead for anything out of the ordinary. I reach the first building and squat against its breezeblock walls. There are no windows or doors on this side. The nearest light is at the foot of the closest main tower, still a long way off. This building is a small shed, barely four metres long. I listen intently. Somewhere, far off, a dog barks. Closer to us a door or a gate swings back and forth in the wind.

Wildgirl eventually makes it to where I'm sitting and crouches next to me, rubbing her elbows and grimacing. Pieces of dried grass cling to her jumper and hair. Her hands are filthy like mine.

'Absolutely no more crawling tonight, and that's a rule. I'm not a slug.'

I want to tell Wildgirl her ukulele is a liability and has to go, but I'm pretty sure she'll tell me where to get off. I creep to the corner of the building. There are four other shed-like structures around us, then a tarmac expanse that looks like a car park. We've done it. We're in Orphanville. I don't know anyone who's been inside these fences. It's time to concentrate, but— 'I'm confused,' I say. I'm confused by the way things turned bad between us. I'm confused by the fact I told her a bunch of personal information and she hasn't said anything about it.

'What about?' Wildgirl presses her chin over my shoulder, trying to see what I'm seeing.

'Do I call you Nia or Wildgirl?'

'Wildgirl, of course. I'm not calling you Jethro, am I?'

I glance back at her. Her lipstick is gone and her eyeshadow is smudged. There's a little crease between her eyebrows that wasn't there before. I did that to her. At the most she was hoping to go to some cool clubs tonight, and maybe see some night-time freaks. Instead I gave her my sob story.

It hurts not having the familiar weight of Gram's lighter in my pocket. It's still a comfort for me to touch something that he so often held. Mum would be so upset if she knew I'd lost it.

I can see the edge of one of the towers at the end of the car park, and beyond it the other towers rising straight in the night. The towers are striped across with windows, and down with a central pillar of light that must be a stairwell or elevator shaft. You can tell from the pattern of lights which buildings are more occupied and more dangerous. Less than a quarter of the lights are on in the closest tower.

It must seem so cool to the Kidds, getting to live together with no parents and no adults and no one telling you what to do. If I'd been younger when the Darkness fell, I wonder if I would have joined them.

'So what was the plan again?' asks Wildgirl.

It took guts to crawl through that fence. I search for my anger but it's gone. She doesn't have to do this, and she doesn't have a gun to my head making me do this either. I owe it to her to make it as easy as possible. It's a pity we haven't thought past 'break in to Orphanville'.

I pull Blake's map from my pocket. It's already wearing thin along the folds. I try to match it up with what lies in front of us, but it morphs into a mess of random writing and scribbles. I sigh. 'I suppose we find Building Six.'

'That's Building Ten, I think.' Wildgirl points at the closest tower. 'The buildings are laid out in two semicircles. One through to Five are on the inside, Six to Ten on the outside.' She pauses, her brow crinkling, her mouth open as if she's about to continue. She takes the map from my hands.

'What is it?' I ask.

'Nothing,' she replies. 'I thought…the placement of the buildings. It's hard to tell.'

'Well, if that's number Ten, the one diagonally behind it is One. Which means Six will be on the left-hand side, right at the end. I think we should go through the middle of the two rows. That way we can go either left or right for cover.'

I stand up and take a few steps away from the shed, so I can see better. The closest towers are mostly dark. Wildgirl was right. We need to work together on this. Maybe it will be easier than we've anticipated. It won't take us long to get to Building Six. We could be in and out in fifteen minutes.

'Careful,' says Wildgirl.

'It's fine,' I say, just as a bright beam of light cuts across my arm and sweeps across my torso. I drop to the ground, half blinded, my vision full of sparkles.

Wolfboy ducks with lightning speed. I flatten myself against the wall, and hold my breath as if it will make a difference to my visibility.

The light sweeps back across the same spot, above where Wolfboy is pressed to the ground, and is gone. I glimpse the tail end of a black car. A narrow driveway, almost invisible from this position, runs behind the car park and in front of the first row of towers. I squint after the car but all I can see is the reflective flash of the number plate. Across to the right is a set of automatic gates closing between two brick pillars. How come we didn't see those before?

When I look back to where Wolfboy was lying just seconds ago there's nothing but fuzzy darkness. He's gone. I'm on the verge of full-blown panic when I see him crouched even further away against Building Ten, waving for me to come over.

Shit. To get there I have to cross the car park and the driveway. I have no idea how Wolfboy covered that distance so fast. The black car is beyond the car park now, but if the driver looks in his rear-vision mirror at the wrong moment he'll see me for sure.

I take a breath then I'm pounding over faded four-square courts painted on the bitumen and dodging a broken soccer net lying on its side. I skid to my knees, scraping against tanbark as I reach Building Ten. It's newer and flashier than the buildings in Plexus Commons, with reflective windows like an office block.

'Do you think they saw us?' I gasp. But we're already away.

Wolfboy drags me by the cuff of my jumper across the narrow gap to the next building. At first I try to resist, but then I just go with him, trying not to fall over or behind. My breath is ragged; white noise fills my ears. The world is a concrete blur. Another tower flashes by. We pass a scrapheap of firewood and mangled bikes. At Building Eight we stop and resume our creeping again.

'What are you doing?' I manage to say. I can't draw enough air into my lungs.

'Come on. I thought I saw something.'

'What?'

I grab his arm and try to hold him back, but he's too strong and I'm forced to follow him to the far corner of the building.

Wolfboy peeks around the corner and then motions for me to come forward. It's not as dark here as I expected. The hazy orange light from the few lampposts dotted around softens the night.

Behind Eight the ribbon of tarmac curves around to the right, running between buildings until it ends in the middle of four towers. A single metal dumpster, five metres away, stands between the road and us. The black car is parked in the dead end with its headlights still on. The doors open, one in the front and one behind, and two men get out. I squint at the buildings beyond the car. I'm not certain yet, but they look—

Wolfboy sneaks even closer to the corner.

'Stop!' I whisper as loudly as I dare. 'Where are you going?'

He slips away, around the corner, where there's barely anything between him and the car and being seen and us being busted and having god knows what done to us.

Shit.

I stick my head around the corner, expecting to see Wolfboy sheltering behind the dumpster. But he's not there. Beyond the dumpster the two men circle to the front of the car. They wear suits and look like secret-service agents, not that I've ever seen one in the flesh.

I take several steps backwards. There's no way I'm following Wolfboy, and I'm not hanging around to see if he's stupid enough to approach the car. I keep backing away until I've rounded another corner. It's possible I'm about to hurl. My head is a messy ball of thoughts, with threads unravelling everywhere. I'm not sure I should have pushed Wolfboy so hard. His family has already lost someone, and let it blow them apart. What if something happens to Wolfboy tonight?

On the other side of Building Eight I stumble across a shallow recess made for a fuse box. The metal box is bolted to the wall, leaving enough room to sit underneath it. It's not the best hiding place but it will do for a few minutes.

I slide into the gap and cuddle my knees to my chest, trying to still my breath and my heart and my hands. This is my punishment for wanting a night that would erase the day, a night with dark secrets and alley chases and passwords. Be careful what you wish for. I close my eyes.

Orphanville feels too real, and at the same time completely unreal, like a dream. There are things going on in this place that I barely understand. Those men could have anything in their boot: guns, or blindfolds, or ropes or bricks. This is not a Kidds' game anymore. We could die here in Orphanville and no one will know what happened to us.

And then the least of my worries will be the girls at school.

My eyes spring open as feet shuffle past. I shrink into the wall. The feet return. Wolfboy drops down next to me, panting and triumphant. 'I knew there was something dodgy about that car!' He looks at me, expecting some kind of pleased reaction, but I give him nothing. 'These two guys got out and talked to some Kidds. The Kidds handed over something in a plastic bag, and then they all got into the car together. I thought they were gonna drive off, but they stayed there. I got closer but I couldn't see anything else. As far as I know they're still there. I bet they've got suitcases full of money.'

He looks at me again, and I blank him.

'Just like a movie...' He stares at me. His head barely clears the fuse box above us. 'What's gotten into you?'

I shrug. 'Nothing.' He doesn't care about the danger he just put himself in.

I do my trick: I go away, out of my head, out of my body, until nothing matters. I am worlds away and I'm not shaking anymore. The night air has frozen me solid; I'm cold and hard all over.

'Don't do this,' Wolfboy says, his voice faint.

'Do what?'

'The cold shoulder. Tell me what I did wrong.' He sounds small and beaten—nothing like the howling boy I met in the pub all those hours ago. It would be easier if he was angry. 'If I knew what I did wrong then I probably wouldn't have done it, would I?'

I breathe out in a thin stream. 'You're not *trying* to get yourself killed, are you?'

Wolfboy gapes.

'What the hell were you doing running after the car like that? We don't know who those people are. Are you trying to get yourself killed?'

I thought I was upset, but my voice sounds angry. I chew my lower lip while Wolfboy looks at me like I'm a grenade with the pin pulled out.

'I thought I recognised the car,' he says, quietly. He doesn't match my anger. 'I went off without thinking, on instinct. I don't have a death wish. Don't think *that*.'

My anger flows out of me as quickly as it came. I wish I could take my words back. I didn't think about what I was suggesting.

'Do you want me to say sorry?'

I think for a few seconds. It wouldn't hurt.

'Yes,' I decide, even though it wasn't that long ago I told him to stop apologising. 'I do.'

'Sorry,' he says genuinely, and for a fraction of a second

I see the little boy in the tree. A warm glow enters my body.

'But I thought this was what you wanted,' Wolfboy says. 'And we've already uncovered something. There's more going on in Orphanville than we suspected.'

I risk a look at him. 'I feel stupid. This was my idea in the first place, but it's much scarier than I thought it would be. At the first sign of danger I run around flapping my hands and you go into action-man mode.'

'I wouldn't worry. You're just getting warmed up.'

I remember suddenly what Blake said at Wolfboy's house. *You don't know what these people are like.* People, not Kidds. She knew there were adults involved.

'It makes sense, doesn't it, that there are adults here?' I say. 'If the Kidds are off their rockers all the time, then there has to be someone straight in charge. And it's not going to be monkeys, is it?'

Wolfboy grins, his incisors white and pointy.

'Did you think we'd find tarsier in the penthouse suite, sitting on stacks of gold bars?'

'Uh-huh. And they'd have giant calculators in their tiny little hands and cocaine on their whiskers.'

We smile at the vision.

Wolfboy puts his hand on my knee. 'I can do this on my own. If you want to turn back, I won't hold it against you. You've done enough already.'

'No. I talked you into this. I'm not backing out now.'

Wolfboy scrambles to his feet and offers me his hand. 'On the positive side, we are now much closer to Building Six.'

'About that,' I say, letting him pull me out from under the fuse box and taking a deep breath. It's time to find out if my suspicions are correct. 'Have you noticed there's something different about Building Seven?'

twenty-one

It's not going to be straight-
forward getting to the other buildings. The car is still
parked in the dead end with its lights off and we don't
know if the men and Kidds are still inside. The break-in
has been worth it just to see the exchange between the
men and the Kidds. It all means something, and I want
to find out what.

'If we double back a bit we'll be out of sight,' whispers
Wildgirl.

I was thinking the same thing.

We go back the way we came until the road straightens
out and the car is no longer visible. I point across the road
to another shed, catch Wildgirl's eye and sketch a path

with my finger. There's not much distance between Seven and Six. We should be able to keep out of view.

The moon sits high above. The scene before us looks flat, as if it has been painted on a canvas with oil paints. The cube-shaped shed. Charcoal smudges of shadow. White highlights from the moon.

We run, keeping low. My backpack bounces up and down. Our feet crunch on the road, then pad through dust to the shed. All other sounds seem to have been sucked from the night.

We huddle behind the shed. I check in with Wildgirl. She smiles tensely in return. I think we're good. It never occurred to me that she would freak out like that. My legs and arms prickle with adrenaline. It's a good feeling. We're really going to do this.

'Ready?' I touch Wildgirl's shoulder, preparing for another burst of running to the back of Seven.

But instead of nodding she clutches my arm. 'What's that sound?'

'What?'

'Listen.'

At first there's only plain grey silence to match the plain grey scene before us, but then I hear it. A faint chattering and a rustle. The barest breath of a breeze floats past us, carrying a definite odour with it.

'I think it's coming from inside—' I don't have to add:

this building. The one we're leaning against.

Wildgirl tightens her grip. I pause, my nostrils taking in the air around us in small puffs. The answer comes to me like a Dreamer in the night.

'Come on,' I whisper. I inch forwards, forcing Wildgirl to loosen her hold. The front of the shed has a narrow verandah and a low wall topped with two chain-link doors. The chattering intensifies. I pull myself up over the edge of the wall to look through the doors. Wildgirl stays at the corner, refusing to come any closer.

Furry lumps cluster in twos and threes on horizontal poles low to the ground and higher up. A heater against the back wall throws off a dull red glow. The air is thick with the musty smell of droppings and urine and fur.

'It's the penthouse suite!' I say, beckoning.

Wildgirl joins me at the ledge.

A few tarsier blink at us, unperturbed. The rest are asleep, some leaning against each other, others sitting in the few scattered branches. I start to count them, but stop at fifty. Wildgirl clings to the mesh, her fingers pushing through the wire.

'They're so teeny. And so peaceful.'

The tarsier seem smaller and more delicate up close. One could sit comfortably in my palm with room to spare. They don't look like they could hurt anyone. A drowsy tarsier slumps on a low perch close to the front. The skin on his fingers is translucent, revealing a spidery network of veins. His paper-thin ears swivel like satellite dishes.

'I've just noticed something,' I say. 'Their eyes don't reflect the light.'

'Are they supposed to?'

'Well, think of dogs or possums or cats. Their eyes all shine at night.'

'No wonder they're so hard to spot in the dark.'

More eyes are opening now; it's as if word has gotten around that there are gawking humans in the neighbourhood.

'How many do you think the Kidds have?'

'No idea. There're a lot here. Maybe they work them in shifts, keep some here to rest while the others do the rounds.'

'Somehow I imagined it differently than that.' Wild-girl watches the tarsier closest to us. She has a tender look on her face, a soft look I haven't seen before. 'I guess I thought they were pets. Like every Kidd has their own little monkey buddy that sits on their shoulders and sleeps on their pillows.'

It's a nice thought. But not a realistic one. 'I've seen some Kidds be pretty horrible to the tarsier. I've seen them get kicked, and thrown, and set alight, you name it,' I say. 'But maybe it's not all one way. Paul has a theory that the tarsier are forming their own army to overthrow the Kidds.'

'I like Paul. When this is all over can we meet up with him again so I can hear all his crackpot theories?'

I look at her, surprised. I don't think a girl has ever willingly spent time with my friends before. 'Sure. But it's not close to over yet, is it?'

'I have an idea.'

Wildgirl examines the doors. A thick chain with a padlock circles the handles. She rattles the chain. Several pairs of eyes open sharply. Dozens of tarsier wriggle, settle down, then wriggle once more.

I think I know what her brilliant idea might be.

'You're not—' I say, and she turns to me.

'It's not locked! They've got this big-arse chain and padlock, and look—' She rattles it again to show it's only looped through the doors and not through the bolt that secures them.

'No. No, you're not.'

'I am.'

'The Kidds will know someone's let them out. They'll know someone's inside Orphanville.'

'If the tarsier get out, they'll be too busy trying to get them back in their cage to worry about where we are. Besides which—ark!'

A tarsier leaps across the enclosure and slams up against the doors, its googly eyes centimetres from Wildgirl's face. She topples backwards, onto her bum.

186

I don't know whether to laugh or tell her to be quiet. She gives me a look that could strip paint, but I can tell even she sees the funny side of it.

'Are you going to help me up or what?'

I help her to her feet. The tarsier is still pressed up against the barricade with a pleading look on his face. His fingers clutch the wire. Several more animals drop to the ground and crawl forward.

'I think he wants to get out,' says Wildgirl, and the tarsier tips his head to the side. 'He does. Poor little fella.'

She extends her index finger, puckering her lips and making kissing sounds. Who would've figured she'd be such a softie? 'It's disgusting what they do to them.'

'You want to lose a finger?' I knock her hand out of the way.

There are dozens of tarsier creeping towards the door now, with love swimming in their eyes. They assemble along the front wall. I swear some of them have their bony hands extended, begging.

'They need us to give them their freedom.'

'How about this? We let them out, and then instead of running away they attack us.'

'Look at them, all cooped up and miserable. It would be really wrong for us to leave them locked up when it's no big deal for us to let them out.'

Wildgirl, moving very deliberately, as if daring me to

stop her, sticks her hand through the gate and draws the bolt across. The tarsier move backwards to make room for the gate's inward swing.

There's a lull for a second, a beat, and then the tarsier swarm as one towards the door. They gush out of the narrow opening and head straight for open ground in every direction, across the car park, up the walls of the nearest building, towards the perimeter fence. They look like ball bearings rolling across the oil-painting landscape.

'Run, little guys!' Wildgirl claps her hands.

I pull her away. We might as well run too.

It's obvious as soon as we make it to Building Seven that Wildgirl is right about it being different: it's at least ten years older than the other towers we've seen. Seven sits on chunky legs painted a faded orange, and has a labyrinthine underbelly of stairs and banisters. A real-life Escher drawing. I preferred the smooth walls of the other buildings. There were fewer places for us to hide, but at least we could see clearly what lay ahead.

Wildgirl seems to have no such qualms. She takes the lead, dragging me along with one woolly hand. She's stuck her thumbs through holes in the sleeves of my jumper, creating makeshift gloves. She's certainly bounced back for someone who was too scared to go any further not ten minutes ago. The building with the bonfire must be close by because I taste smoke in the air.

We go up a short flight of stairs and follow the building around to the left. The walls are made from thousands of glittering rocks glued together with concrete. We're going in the wrong direction, away from Six. I rack my brains for a nice way to say this to Wildgirl.

'This is perfect,' Wildgirl says.

'What is?'

'These buildings are built on the same plan as Plexus Commons.'

We pass a stairwell with a locked cage full of bikes underneath it. Plexus Commons? I must look confused because she says, 'I told you. I live in a housing project. There are eight buildings in the Commons, where I live, and they're all exactly the same, inside and out. Well, Orphanville must have been built on the same plan, 'cause I know my way around here like it's the back of my hand. The buildings up this end must have been built before the others.'

'Are you sure? Maybe they just look the same on the outside.'

Wildgirl strides out in her cowboy boots like the footpath is a catwalk. Two lit-up windows on the first level watch us like a pair of yellow eyes. Other windows are propped open to let air in, and sound. Unlike the others, this building feels lived in. Wildgirl stops and faces me. At least she has the good sense to keep her voice down.

'Ask me how many floors this building has.'

'We don't have time for this.'

'There are twelve. Did you see me look up and count them at any point?'

'All right, all right.' I hold my hands up in defeat. 'But what's wrong with running across to Six? We can make it there in seconds.'

'Because that's not the plan. Just trust me.'

I can't help myself. 'Sure. If you trust me, that is.'

Her eyes flare like struck matches.

'Oh, are we going to have this conversation now?' she says.

I take her woolly hand in mine again. I could jog her memory about her death-wish comment, but I keep it to myself. It's too good having her by my side. We should save our fury for when we need it.

'Later. Tell me how we're getting into Six.'

22

What Wolfboy doesn't know is that the way into Six is through Seven. And the way into Seven is straight through the front door as if we are sherbet-snorting, lollypop-sucking Kidds. I won't lie; the sunken entrance looks like a hellmouth, but I force myself down the stairs.

The glass doors are smeared with the prints of a thousand Kiddy fingers. The foyer is deserted and no warmer than outside. Harsh fluorescent lights bounce off the worn lino floor and fake wood panels. The decor is different, but I'm almost a hundred per cent certain the layout of these buildings will match that of the Commons.

I march straight to the elevator and press the up button.

I know what our next few moves should be, and I want Wolfboy to regain his confidence in me. No more hysteria. Letting the tarsier out wasn't the smartest thing to do, but it also meant I'm not scared anymore to do the right thing. I don't think it's harmed our chances. Not yet anyway.

The elevator doesn't arrive. I cross my arms and fiddle with the ragged ends of my sleeves. I may know where we're going but I still don't know what we're going to find there. I notice Wolfboy is looking on edge again, so I force myself to stop fidgeting. I don't blame him. We're sitting ducks here, highlighted in sickly fluorescent.

'What do we do when we see someone?' asks Wolfboy. 'They're gonna know straightaway that we don't belong here. We need a story. Or are we going to shoot first, ask questions later?'

I press the up button again and focus on the row of floor numbers above the elevator doors, pretending I can make it arrive quicker by staring at them. Come on. Why can't I even hear it moving?

'We need to play it by ear. I recommend we don't come out with all guns blazing. We should try to talk our way out of things first.'

The elevator finally begins its descent. The floor numbers light up in turn: 5, 4, 3, 2, 1.

'It was just sitting on the fifth floor,' I point out. 'That's a good sign.'

The lift hits the ground floor with a clunk. Wolfboy's boots squeak on the lino as he crouches in a defensive stance. I fix my eyes on the steel doors, preparing for whatever is behind them. The doors open.

The lift is empty.

It's lit by one weak bulb and smells seriously nasty, of urine or something worse. There's a beaten-up old stool in one corner and every wall is tagged in red texta. It's gross, but empty.

The doors close loudly behind us. The elevator is rickety and draughty and I'm pretty sure I can see gaps where the walls join the floor. I press the top button, marked 'R'. The cables and weights that operate the deathtrap clunk around us. These walls are as flimsy as cardboard.

'R?'

'Roof.'

'Are we going to abseil to Six?'

'We need to look at the lie of the land before we rush in. We'll be able to see everything from the roof. See any traps. Plot some escape routes.'

Wolfboy goes quiet so I guess he thinks my plan isn't completely insane. There's one thing I can't accuse him of, and that's being all alpha and macho. He was listening when I said we had to be a team. And right now this team member needs to go up to the roof to clear her mind. When we crossed the fence into Orphanville we didn't leave our problems behind us, but once we're in Building Six, with a chance to get the lighter, I don't want to be thinking about anything else.

I turn my attention to the numbers above the door.

2.

3.

The passage of the elevator is far from smooth and several times it lurches and halts, only to jerk upwards a second later.

4.

5.

'It's a bit like Russian roulette, isn't it?' I say, without losing sight of the floor numbers as they light up.

'Losing your nerve?' he says, but I suspect he's scared rigid. I'm probably only seconds away from totally losing it myself. Please don't let the elevator stop. Please let it go straight to the roof.

And then it happens.

8.

The elevator stops.

DING!

I only have time to swear once before the doors open.

The eighth floor is pitch-black and it's impossible to see anything beyond the elevator mouth. A figure shuffles out of the dark. Wolfboy moves into the back corner of the lift. I guess he took on board the whole no-guns-blazing thing.

A short Kidd enters, carrying a mini TV with a cracked screen. His windcheater hood obscures almost his entire face, and his bare feet are scratched and filthy. A stench like wet wool and chicken manure fills the elevator.

He shuffles in without looking at us, turns to face the doors and presses number 11. He wears a plank of wood strapped diagonally across his back like a sword. My eyes widen. Shards of glass have been glued to the wood with their points facing up. If anyone was unlucky enough to get hit with it, they'd bleed in about fifty different places. The doors slam shut and the elevator creaks into action once more.

9.

I don't breathe. Keep calm. I wriggle my shoulders so I can feel the ukulele shift. If necessary I will sacrifice it on any Kidd that needs a ukulele to the head.

Hoodie can't stand still; he tap-dances on the lino. Chances are he can't see us clearly under his hood, or he's too high to care. The stool legs bang on the floor as the elevator moves. Hoodie turns towards us in response to the sound, and grunts a greeting. He holds the TV forward.

'Losht my power privilegesh,' he says with a killer lisp. 'Gordie took my stash sho I knife him.'

Neither of us speaks.

It's obviously not the pleasant elevator conversation Hoodie is looking for because he tenses up and swings around to face us. His face could be half melted away under that hood and we wouldn't know. A hand lets go of the TV and sneaks over his shoulder to touch the tip of his makeshift weapon.

I glance over at Wolfboy and he's frozen against the corner.

It's up to me.

I curl in on myself and think short thoughts. I fold my shoulders forwards and rock back and forth on my heels. I make my eyes wondrous and bite on my lip.

'Sounds like Gordie got what he deserved,' I say in a voice that's more than half-Chipmunk. I think I've overdone it, but Hoodie grins, exposing nothing but mottled pink gums. No wonder he talks like he's got a mouth full of fairy floss. His twitching hand drops and he grapples with the TV for a few seconds, trying not to drop it.

'Haven't finish wiv him yet though, have I?'

11.

The elevator jerks and Hoodie shifts his hands on the TV to get a better grip.

'What'sh wiv the'—he gestures with the TV— 'What'sh wiv the bow-wow-wow?'

Oh, Wolfboy's going to love that.

'Oh him?' I twirl a piece of hair around my finger, and

try to sound clueless. 'Dunno. Boss says I gotta take care of him. He's a freelancer or something.'

The doors open. Hoodie nods sagely. I catch a flash of his shiny eyes as his hood slips.

'Bit of dat going on these daysh. Dey caught a no name out tonight, sho there might be bit of ackshon. I hope.'

No name. That's what the barman said at Little Death when I was using the card.

The eleventh floor reeks of smoke and pulses with red light. As Hoodie crosses the threshold he stumbles and drops to his knees. The TV falls from his hands and crashes to the floor. A shard of black plastic flies off into the darkness. Wolfboy rushes forward to help as Hoodie rolls onto his side and curls into a protective ball.

Something makes me throw my arm out, stopping Wolfboy from leaving the elevator. I have just enough time to glimpse a second figure lying in wait, in the hallway, before the doors slam shut.

23

My heart still isn't back to its normal rhythm when the elevator spits us out at the last floor. The steel doors open onto a vestibule, and I half-run up the narrow flight of steps towards the roof. The stairs end at a hospital-green door. Everything is exactly where it should be.

'Slowly,' Wolfboy warns me as I press down on the handle. I push the door open gradually, peering into the biting night air.

The rooftop is empty. I take Wolfboy's hand, more for my comfort than his. The rooftop is a flat concrete rectangle; maybe thirty metres by twenty. A waist-high wall encloses it. At the Commons this isn't high enough to discourage the occasional jumper; I wonder if they have the same problem in Orphanville.

My nostrils twitch with the acrid smell of burnt wood. Someone has been engaging in some serious pyromania up here. The rooftop is littered with charred wood; the concrete is scarred with scorch marks and smears of charcoal. A stack of burnt furniture is in the centre. It could be my imagination, but the concrete feels warm under my feet.

Everyone that lives in the Commons has the right to use the rooftop of their own building, but in reality there's always a group of people in each building that controls it. Mine is lorded over by a gang of card-playing, gin-drinking grandmas who don't mind me. So I could go up there if I wanted to, but I haven't in years.

I drop Wolfboy's hand and go to the edge to see this strange dark suburb from up high. I need to be alone for a moment. I lean on the concrete barricade and fill my lungs with fresh air. My foggy breath gets carried away on the breeze. I look down at the frill of trees around Orphanville and the snaking river, and then I lift my eyes to the velvet sky. The city beneath me could easily be the sky's reflection: an endless blackness scattered with pinpricks of light.

There it is.

That familiar feeling, like a sunburst might explode

from my chest, like a wave might splash over me and wash me clean. When I used to look from the roof of my building in the Commons, my whole body would tingle as I saw my world from above. Not because of what was directly below me, but what was beyond the edges of my vision. The world. A whole world out there, bigger and better than I could imagine.

Here, on this rooftop, the world around me is foreign. I imagine tarsier specks racing away in the darkness, spreading out to the river and the streets and the backyards. I drink the view in until I'm dizzy and could sail away with the wonder of it all. Trying to hold on to this feeling is like trying to keep water cupped in your hands. All you can do is preserve it for as long as possible.

'I'm not afraid.' I speak out loud without meaning to. Wolfboy is still standing where I dropped his hand. 'Come have a look.'

'I'm not good with heights.'

'Neither am I, but it doesn't even look real from up this high.'

We stand together, his arm pressing against mine.

'What do you think is down there?' I ask.

'Pete and Thom somewhere, drinking and talking shit. People getting into fights, Kidds causing trouble. Lupe asleep at her table.' He falls quiet for a few seconds and then he makes a slow whistling sound.

'No howling?' If I could howl then that's what standing on this roof would do to me.

'That would give us away, don't you think?'

Right. Excellent point.

'You can see Panwood from here.' He points to where the lights are gathered in orderly rows. They grow thicker at the edges of the view.

'And other parts of the City.' I point to the skyscraper with its top floors encased in gold. 'The Golden Finger.'

'Is that what it's called?'

'That's what I call it. It's probably got some corporate name. I see it on my way to school. Sometimes it flashes beams of light if the sun's right. I've always thought the people who built it are secretly flipping the bird to the whole city.'

'It's been so long since I've thought about what happens outside Shyness.'

'My life would bore you to tears.'

'I don't think so. I get the feeling you don't live your life in an ordinary way. Like you could be doing your homework at your desk and it would be an adventure for you.'

'I don't have a desk. There's no room. I do my home-work at the kitchen table.'

'Well, you know what I mean anyway.'

I smile at him. There's admiration in his voice. I don't

know if I deserve it. But when all I usually hear is that I'm too loud, too argumentative, too opinionated, too impulsive, too tactless, too talkative, *too much* of anything, then I'll take whatever compliments I can get.

'You're different, aren't you?'

He barks out a laugh. 'You only realised that now?'

'I mean you're different now from when we first met. You know, when I first saw you at the pub, I thought you were some wannabe rock star: way too cool for your own good. I didn't want to be impressed by you, but I was. But you're not at all. Cool, that is.'

'Thanks…I think.'

'You're different from the boys at home. I don't think I've met anyone like you before.'

I should think of something specific to say here, but I don't want to be corny. And then I surprise myself with what comes out of my mouth next.

'I'm glad you told me about your brother.'

Wolfboy looks at me, confused, and I don't blame him for failing to see the connection. I didn't mean to bring his brother up again.

'I can't really imagine what that would be like,' I add, as if it will clear things up.

'I wouldn't want you to know what it was like.'

'The only person I've lost was my nan.'

Even though I knew I'd miss her, I didn't feel so bad

when Nan died. She was ready. She said so herself. Nan was the link between my mum and me. After she went, Mum and I were cut off from each other, floating around our flat like astronauts in deep space.

'You know Ortolan,' Wolfboy says, 'the woman we talked to at the Raven's Wing? I don't know if she told you, but she's, I mean, was—'

'She was your brother's girlfriend.' When I found out Gram was dead it made sense the way Ortolan looked at Wolfboy, and how she seemed both frail as a bird and steely-strong at the same time.

'What else did she tell you?'

'Not much else,' I say. There's no need to mention the things Paul told me.

'Ortolan lives over the border, in Panwood.' He points again at the cluster of lights. 'But I hardly ever see her. I don't avoid her, but I don't make any effort either.'

'Do you blame her for what happened to Gram?'

'No, of course not. But she's part of the past. We've probably got nothing in common. She's got a child to take care of. And she's this fancy fashion designer now—'

'She didn't seem unhappy to see you at the Raven's Wing. Just a bit awkward. If you wanted to be back in her life I'm sure you could be.'

'I made a fool of myself earlier.'

He looks so young in this moment that I know that's

exactly what he wants even if he doesn't know it, to be in touch with a piece of life before the Darkness.

He straightens up, lifts his elbows off the wall. 'So, what do we need to notice from here?'

We've slipped sideways again in the night, losing focus on what's going on around us, like in the Dreamer room at the club. I force my attention back to the buildings below. From here it's like a living map, everything laid out neatly around us.

'First of all, we should take note of everything that's around Building Six. We need to know the quickest escape route, and, failing that, all the other ways of getting the hell out of here. Can we look at the map?' By the time we leave the Kidds could be on our heels.

'The main gates are the closest exit,' Wolfboy says.

'Are they manned?' Wolfboy's eyesight must be twice as good as mine. I can't even see the gates in the gloom.

'I doubt it. No one but Kidds would want to go through there.'

'If we're cut off from the main entrance then we'll have to run back the way we came. Through the hole in the fence again.'

'Not necessarily. There's the back gates. As long as the car's here those gates should stay open. If they were going to close them they would have done it straight-away.'

I check. The black car is still parked between the buildings.

Wolfboy frowns at the open space between this building and the next. 'We're gonna have to fang it across to Six. There are probably Kidds around every corner.'

'We don't need to worry,' I say. The other part of my plan will take care of that.

'I'm glad you're feeling confident.' Wolfboy is getting restless. 'Are you ready to go?'

I grab one of his hands and pancake it between mine. His eyes are so dark, I think of the impossibility of ever *really* knowing him.

'One more thing. See all this...' I look up at the stars and the lights and the velvety night and the strange, strange world. 'This is all we have, just this. Just now.'

He's not with me. I keep trying.

'All we have is this feeling, right here, right now. Nothing else exists. Nothing really matters.'

I'm still not sure he gets it.

I skim my hands over his hair; I imagine silver threads running from my fingers as I wrap my hands around his face, still barely touching him. I have a moment of terror when I realise how much I like him. This isn't like crushing on someone from a distance.

'I release you,' I whisper, half joking, half serious. 'From the past and the future and all the boring ad breaks.'

I wish these things for myself as well. I really, really wish these things for myself.

Wolfboy takes one of my hands and holds it to his lips. He's standing so close I can feel the heat from his body. I force myself to step away. I don't want to start something we're going to have to stop. I wish it could be just him and me hiding from the world somewhere quiet. But it's time for business.

twenty-four

The lift is still there when we come off the roof. It shoots down to the basement of Seven without stopping. The elevator doors open onto a frigid and dark corridor. I don't bother asking Wildgirl where we're going. She's kooky, that's for sure, but I'm willing to trust her. No one else I know could have talked their way out of that situation in the lift, and it did help seeing Orphanville from up high.

Wildgirl turns left, her fingers moving along the wall for guidance. It can't be easy for her in this darkness. I half-close my eyes, trying to get an idea of what it's like.

We take a short flight of stairs down further into the dark and hit a concrete stub of a corridor that smells of piss. Cold leaches from the walls. A dim blue light shines through a metal grate low on the wall, at foot-level. There are four rusty washing machines against the opposite wall, one with the lid ripped off. For a second I think the black hose coiled on the floor is a snake. I give up squinting before I give myself a headache or a heart attack. Wildgirl inspects one of the broken machines.

'Fact Number One. Kidds do not like to do laundry. Yet another reason why we should give them a wide berth this evening.'

The only way to get out of this dead end is to go back exactly the same way we came.

'I give up. How are we getting to Six?'

Wildgirl points to the grate. It has chunky metal bars that latch onto the wooden frame underneath.

'You want me to bend those apart?' I ask. 'It's flattering you think I can do that, but—'

Wildgirl sighs melodramatically, kicks the grate hard on each side, then kneels and removes it. It comes away easily, in one piece. She holds it up, smirking, then leans it against the wall.

'Sir, your safe passage to Building Six is secured.'

I peer through the rectangular hole. 'What's down there?'

'Are you scared?'

'Actually, yes. I wouldn't mind knowing if we're about

208

to drop into…I don't know, a sugarlab, or a vat of acid.'

'It's a service tunnel. There's a network of underground passages that connect all the buildings. Well, the older ones at least. I'd bet my favourite handbag on it.' She slaps her forehead. 'Oh, but hang on, we gave that one away already, didn't we?'

I ignore her. I'm going to replace her bag later if I can. Maybe Sebastien can help me out.

'So, we should be able to get into Six's basement?'

'That's the idea. Ninja-style.' She kneels in front of the hole and sticks her head through. I look away. Perving won't help me now.

'It's all clear down here. Are you ready?'

I guess so.

'I'll go first; it's not much of a drop.'

She reverses through the gap, shimmying down until she's balanced on her stomach.

'Here goes.' She drops. I hear her feet scuff against the floor below, and a discordant twang from the ukulele.

'You all right?' I call out. The last thing we need right now is a sprained ankle or broken bone.

'Yep.' Her voice is echoey and distant, even though she can't be more than a few metres away.

I post my backpack through the hole first. Disembodied hands pull it from me. I wait a few seconds and then I slide through. It's going to be a much tighter squeeze for me.

My hands are still gripping the ledge when my feet hit solid ground. The service tunnel is only a few metres wide, with rough walls and a low ceiling. Fat metal pipes run along the right-hand side of the tunnel. Skinnier pipes and bundles of cables run overhead. A strip light interrupts the darkness every five metres or so. The air is stale, but surprisingly warm.

'So this is what you do for fun in Plexus? Crawl through the sewers?'

Wildgirl hands my bag back.

'There's no sewage down here. It's mostly heating ducts and power cables. I've only been in the tunnels a few times at home, but my friend used them all the time. He could get from one side of Plexus to the other without seeing daylight.'

She doesn't say his name, but I know she means the friend she mentioned earlier, Mike.

The tunnel forks into two identical tunnels ahead of us.

'We're going to get lost under here, aren't we?' I look back up at the opening. If necessary I can boost Wildgirl, and then lift myself through.

'Nope.' Wildgirl's voice is firm. 'Six is definitely in this direction. The other tunnel must connect to Four. The tunnels in the Commons are on a grid so there's no reason to think these aren't the same.'

I have to stoop as we take the tunnel to the left. The pipes are old and covered in grime. Heat fuzzes from them and they creak like snoring babies. Every now and then there's a wheel or a lever or a hazard sign to break the monotony. Our feet crunch on the dry concrete floor. I adjust my bag, settling the weight evenly between my shoulders.

'I wonder if these connect to the old subway tunnels near Little Death.'

'Maybe.'

'We should be leaving markers in case we get lost and have to turn around.'

Wildgirl doesn't answer me. The acoustics in here are good. I feel like I'm whispering but my voice is loud. You could record some amazing stuff down here if you could figure out how to tap some electricity. We pass a manhole overhead, with a metal ladder fixed to the wall underneath it.

I hope this isn't a waste of time. At least we're hidden down here, and Wildgirl does seem to know her way around. Maybe a lot of government buildings are built the same, to save money.

'So, do you like where you live?' I ask.

'It's a dump,' Wildgirl says without turning back. 'We live in a tiny apartment about the size of your front room. All around us there are hundreds of other people living in apartments exactly the same as ours. Everyone stacked on top of each other. We have our own bathroom and kitchen but we have to share a laundry and rubbish bins and car park. I can't wait to get out of there.'

Oh. Her steps speed up, forcing me to pick up my pace. Her voice sounds odd, maybe because of the acoustics.

'What about your school?' I ask.

'I go to a private school on a scholarship. You know, the smart poor kid. There's one in every school. The girls there own at least ten pairs of jeans each and three times as many pairs of shoes, and I've been wearing the same uniform since I started there. They think I like to wear my school dress short.'

She laughs, but it's not light. She must hate me after seeing my house. I know I haven't been keeping it like my mum used to, but still. It must be obvious we have—had—money. That stuff shouldn't make a difference though, right? Am I supposed to apologise that my parents are well off?

A sudden boom clangs through the tunnel. I'm so shocked I jump and slam into the pipes next to me. There's a loud hiss, and a few metres further on a cloud of steam escapes into the air. Hair stands up all over my body.

When the steam clears I see Wildgirl ahead, waiting for me with her arms crossed, smirking.

'The pipes do that sometimes,' she says.

I dust myself off and join her. My body is crawling with unwanted adrenaline. The moment calls for pretend dignity, so that's exactly what I give her. I put on a poncy British accent. 'Where I come from, our pipes are solid gold. With diamonds. Father said I can have one for my birthday if I'm lucky.'

She laughs and punches me on the shoulder. Who says I can't act?

'Houston, we have a problem.'

She's right. Up ahead there's a barred gate blocking our way. It's been made to fit the uneven contours of the tunnel, wrapping around the bulge of pipes on one side. It's secured by a latch with an old-fashioned keyhole. I try the handle but it's locked. I grab the door with both hands and shake it. Nothing doing.

'You know,' Wildgirl says, 'I think I might be able to squeeze through.'

The bars are spaced barely fifteen centimetres apart. My scepticism shows.

'Not the bars, stoopid. The side—here.' Wildgirl pokes her arms through the gap where the gate accommodates the pipes. There's a decent space between pipes and gate. Still...

'I don't think you're gonna fit through that.'

'I'm not that fat,' she says. 'God! Way to make a woman feel special, *Jethro*.'

'Did I say—' I start, and then stop. I know when I'm not going to win an argument. 'Let me try to break the lock first.'

'No need,' says Wildgirl. She strips off her jumper—make that my jumper—and flings it through the bars. It lands out of reach on the other side. I notice she doesn't take the same risk with the ukulele, placing it carefully against the wall.

She gets her right arm and shoulder easily through. Her head scrapes by, barely, then her hips. 'Oof!' she gasps. She's done it. She puts the jumper back on and holds on to the gate with both hands, mocking me. Her hair is wild.

'Come on then, action man.'

Gram used to do this thing where he'd ask me to shut the front gate while he waited in the car, then, when I tried to open the passenger door to get in, he'd inch the car forward in infuriating lurches so I couldn't. Same annoying principle.

'I'm waiting.'

'There's no way I'm getting through there.'

'Then you're lucky you've got me.'

Wildgirl bends down to look at the latch and the keyhole. 'It's jammed from this side. Someone's put a piece of cardboard or something in here. Can you pass my make-up bag? It's in your front pocket.'

I find a zebra-striped toiletry bag and pass it through the bars.

Wildgirl uses a pair of tweezers to remove a wad of cardboard from the lock and then rummages again in her make-up bag.

'Voila.' She pulls out a hairpin and sits cross-legged with her bag in her lap. I pace down the corridor the way we came and peer into the distance. Nothing. Just the tap and groan of the pipes.

'Any time now,' I say. 'Any second a flood of psycho children may come through that hole, but, you know, take your time.'

Wildgirl doesn't look up from her task. She's bending a hairpin out of shape.

'How old is Ortolan's kid?' she asks out of nowhere.

I blink. 'I don't know. She had her while she was overseas.'

'Which was after she and Gram split up, right? Which was how long ago?'

I have to stretch my mind to remember. Everything's a blur. Nothing from before seems real.

'You're the one who's seen a photo of her.' I manage to keep the care-factor out of my voice, but Wildgirl still looks up. 'What do you think?'

'Maybe four or five years old. And how long ago did Ortolan break up with Gram?'

'Maybe five years ago…' The words are sluggish in my mouth. Ideas uncoil, oily and slow like eels.

'And you've all been living in the dark for almost as long.'

Wildgirl's eyes meet mine, then she looks down again. She sticks the bent hairpin into the lock and then removes it, working it into the right shape.

If your girlfriend got pregnant to another man, you'd be pretty upset. You'd have to break up and everything you'd planned for your future would be up in smoke. It wouldn't seem as if you had much to live for in those circumstances.

Gram was only nineteen. Next year I'll be the same age as he was when he died. And the year after that I'll be older than he ever was. I used to think he was a man, used to think he knew everything, but he was barely an adult when he had to cope with all these problems. I can barely deal with anything more complicated than eating and sleeping.

'My mum has never told me who my dad is,' Wildgirl says. 'He could be anyone. Best-case scenario is this: they were young and he was scared. My mum couldn't go through with an abortion, and he couldn't go through with being a dad. So he ran. Refused to have anything to do with it. With us, I mean, with me.'

Wildgirl's arms are by her sides, her make-up bag

and tools on the dusty ground in front of her. Her eyes are liquid and big.

'Worst-case scenario,' I reply. 'She pushed him away, she refused to let him have anything to do with it.' But I'm thinking about Ortolan, not Wildgirl, and I'm adding and subtracting in my mind.

Wildgirl's face is scrunched up with something like pain and I'm sure mine is the same, but I didn't mean to be cruel. Wildgirl kneels in front of the lock and tries the hairpin. The pin scrapes against the metal and I hear a click. Wildgirl presses down on the handle and the gate moves.

'We don't know, do we?' she says quietly. The gate creaks open, wiping an arc in the dust as it swings. The sound it makes is a rusty wail.

I walk through. The tunnel looks exactly the same on the other side. Same pipes, same lights on the roof. I take Wildgirl's hand and hold it so tightly I can feel a faint pulse in her fingers. She looks up at me and her smile is strangely grateful. Our words have hurt each other but we didn't mean them to. The truth hurts, but not knowing the truth hurts more.

twenty-five

The basement in Six is almost identical to Seven's, except instead of washing machines there's a collection of cardboard boxes and a rotting mattress in the corner. A single hanging bulb lights the corridor at the top of the déjà vu stairs.

'If I was going to have a safe room,' I remark, 'I would put it in a separate purpose-built building, with a moat and armed security guards and an electric fence.'

'Then everyone would know exactly where you kept your best stuff. And that's the first place they'd attack. With the biggest army they could muster.'

'Didn't you hear me? Gunmen? A *moat*?'

Wildgirl rolls her eyes, refusing, for a change, to

play along. 'There are twelve floors in every building. Didn't Blake say around ten units live in each building?' I nod. 'So, they need to set aside ten rooms. You'd definitely use a spare floor, at either the top or bottom of the building. Let's search this level, and then switch to the top level and work our way down. That way the longer we've been in here—'

I interject. 'And the more likely it is that they're gonna find us—'

Wildgirl jumps in, nodding. 'Then the closer we'll be to the ground floor, and our escape route.'

There are two doors on each side of the corridor before the elevator shaft. Without the need for further discussion I take the left-hand side and Wildgirl does the right.

The first door I try leads into a storage closet containing a cache of plastic jerry cans and a suffocating smell of petrol. I pull the door shut, and move on to the next one.

'They're not down here,' I call out. 'There are no locks on the doors, and everything's dusty. No one's been this way for a while.'

The next door opens onto disused sports equipment: spongy basketballs, tangled nets, an old wooden vaulting horse. Nothing useful.

'I think you're right,' she says, 'but at least I got this.'

I turn around to find her in a fencing stance and swishing a green gardening fork. Her movements send doppelganger shadows flashing across the walls.

'It's my trident. Nice, huh?'

'Lethal. Did you find anything for me?'

'Of course. I wouldn't forget you.'

She holds up a small spade with a metal scoop and a short wooden handle.

'A trowel?' My voice still goes squeaky when I'm indignant. 'Behold, the awesome might of my *trowel*?'

She throws it at me and I catch it with one hand. It looks like a teaspoon in my hands. I fit it into a mesh pocket on the side of my backpack.

'You're right, there's sweet eff-all down here. Let's head to the top.'

Wildgirl marches past the elevator and opens the last door. There is a large '6' painted on it, so there's no doubt anymore that we're in the right building. Wildgirl props the door open with a foot and gestures for me to follow. Cold air wafts through the open door.

'No elevator?' I ask.

'I've gone off it. We'll take the stairs instead. If we hear anyone coming we can go up or down a level and duck through a door.'

The stairwell extends high above us. I peer up through the central gap, all the way to the top of the building, and get reverse vertigo. The stairs are divided into half-flights, with a small landing at the halfway point, and then a larger landing at each floor. A frosted window on each main landing lets in dim moonlight.

We climb side-by-side, wordlessly. Wildgirl has tucked the garden fork into her belt loop. I settle into the climb, glancing across at her occasionally. Every now and then a pale stripe of moonlight cuts across her face. Neither of us has mentioned what we talked about in the tunnels. It's as if it never happened. Maybe what goes on underground stays underground.

'You're miles away. What are you thinking about?' I ask.

'I was thinking about revenge.'

'On the Kidds?'

'No. Not the Kidds.'

'Then who?' I ask, but she doesn't reply.

The problem with Gram's death was that there wasn't anyone to blame except for him, and he wasn't around to take it. I know my parents went dark on Ortolan, or at least my father did. If I was forced to pick sides I would have put the blame closer to home.

'What level do you think we're up to?'

Wildgirl's cheeks are pink and she's short of breath.

'Coming up to Seven,' she says. 'I've been keeping count.'

I stop. 'That's the Elf's home floor. Why don't we take a quick look?'

'Too dangerous. We know they were heading for home

a while ago, so we could walk right into their clutches.'

'We don't know for sure that the safe rooms exist. If for some chance they're there with the lighter, we could negotiate.'

Of course there's no way the Elf would give up the lighter for a plastic bag full of garden-variety chocolate bars, but there are other things we could bargain with, no matter what Blake thinks. I know people in Shyness who can get you whatever you want, at a price. Or I could offer my own services.

'Don't you think your friend Blake tried to reason with them? And look what happened to her.'

Wildgirl climbs again, her boots making way too much noise on the concrete stairs.

I give up. I'm supposed to be the one who knows how Shyness operates, but it occurs to me that we're acting on a bunch of second-hand information. From people who may or may not be trustworthy. Maybe we need to quit the subterfuge and ask the next Kidd we see where the Elf is. Deal with him directly.

At the top of the stairwell I glance down at all the floors we've passed. If we have to get out fast, it will be straight back down here. I judge the distance between flights. I could vault over the railing and take half a flight of stairs at a time, but I'm not sure Wildgirl could do the same.

Wildgirl stands in front of the final door.

'When we go through this door, there will be the elevator to our right, and stairs to the rooftop on the left, same as the other building. To get to the main corridor we go through a glass door on the right, beyond the elevator.'

I picture it, trying to fix the layout in my head.

'Ready?'

I push past Wildgirl, and press my weight against the door. She may be calling the shots, but I can at least take the first blow when it comes.

The twelfth floor glows with purple light from two UV lamps positioned at either end of the corridor. I hit the locking mechanism at the top of the glass door to keep it open. Someone has stuck rows and rows of different coloured electrical tape along the length of the floor, making a rainbow. I move forwards on the balls of my feet, hugging the wall. The ceiling and walls are painted black, with silver stars that glow.

Wildgirl follows close behind. We pass a door on our right: there's a faint throb of music behind it. Wildgirl raises her hand to the handle and I shake my head. We keep sliding forwards. The next door, on our left, is bolted and padlocked. I could get a screwdriver out of my bag and have a go at it, but I think we're better off seeing what the other rooms hold.

Wildgirl lays her ear against the next door and nods. She steps back and I open the door onto a room bathed in moonlight. There's a clump of blankets on the floor, a cache of spray cans in a box, a death-metal poster tacked to the wall and a terrible stench. I hold my nose, walk inside and take a cursory look around. Off the main room there's a kitchen full of lab equipment, and a festering bathroom. Another tiny room contains a blow-up mattress and a sleeping bag.

It looks like we're on an ordinary residential floor. The next few doors are unlocked. One opens onto an empty apartment with a burnt-out kitchen. The next is stocked heavily for entertainment. The bedroom has a wall-to-wall stereo system instead of a bed. The kitchen is unused. The corridor ends in an open smoking room. I use one finger to indicate we should do a U-turn. Wildgirl backtracks but stops again at the door with the bolt and padlock.

I stare at the bolt, assessing the risk. It looks flimsy. I could probably get the screws out fairly quickly. But if it was a safe room wouldn't it be secured better than this? Wildgirl puts her hand on my arm, about to say something, when there's a thump at the end of the corridor.

The elevator.

I don't have time to think.

I pull her by the hand and we run up the corridor towards the stairwell beyond the elevator. We've only got a second or two, at the most. We're just through the glass doorway when there's a ding.

The elevator doors slide open and we stand in front of it, momentarily shocked into stopping. Three suited men look back at us, and, towering palely in the corner, is the Elf.

Wildgirl grabs my arm and pulls me away. She hurtles up the steel steps to the rooftop and I have no choice but to follow her. We're out in the night air, looking around frantically before I even have time to consider how trapped we are.

twenty-six

Another concrete rectangle bounded by a concrete wall, with the black sky above, and only one door in and out. The men in suits and the Elf can only be a few metres away on the other side of the door. My hand jams the handle upwards, so it can't be pressed down on the other side. We look at each other with dinner-plate eyes.

'Quick.'

I have no thoughts other than getting away from the door and finding a good place to hide. We dodge stacked paint tins and crumpled tarpaulins and canvas sheets spattered with colour. We need something tall. I leap over a discarded typewriter and take a split-second look back.

The door swings open and the three men and the Elf step onto the roof. The suits fan out around the doorway. The Elf hangs back, silhouetted against falling yellow light.

I pull Wildgirl down behind an upright ladder draped with a sheet. Not ideal, but good enough. We're almost as far away as we can get from the men, huddled in the back corner of the roof.

I peek through the rungs. A rip in the sheet frames one of the suited men perfectly. He stands statue-still and switches his gaze from place to place efficiently. Sunglasses cover half his face. I don't think he's one of the men I saw earlier at the car but there's something familiar about him. He gestures for one of the other men to circle around the back of the stairwell, and the second to check in our direction. The way he stands suggests that he's more than just a security guard.

I look around, seeing if there's anything within arm's reach. A bucket full of paint rollers won't be much use. Nor will a pile of old egg cartons. Could I use the ladder to make a bridge to the neighbouring tower? No. Far too dangerous. Wildgirl crouches lower than me, looking around the side of the ladder. She unhooks the garden fork from her waist and stares at the sunglasses man.

'I know that guy,' she whispers. She tugs on my jeans. Her mouth is open with surprise. 'It's Doctor Gregory!'

I look through the rip in the sheet.

She's right. He's removed his sunglasses now—it's definitely him. He looks like a different person in a suit and long black overcoat, with his ginger hair slicked back. The orange tan is still in place, but the cheesy grin has turned grim. Smooth on the outside and rotten underneath.

My skin prickles all over. Doctor Gregory. It makes perfect sense that he's involved with the Kidds and Orphanville. First you create the problem, and then you sell everyone the solution.

Doctor Gregory steps forward as if he knows that we're looking at him. As if he's on the set of another motivational video.

'Is this what you're looking for?'

His voice rings out clearly despite the open air and whistling breeze. He holds a small silver object above his head with a thumb and index finger. It looks like my lighter, but I don't trust him. He swivels from side to side, holding the lighter up high, making sure we don't miss it, wherever we are.

'Would you like it?' Doctor Gregory's voice is steel-hard and nothing like the voice he uses in his videos. 'You must really want it to go to these lengths. I admire that. I don't think young people should be punished for showing such initiative.'

My eyes are fixed on the lighter. It's not as bright as the flashy watch buckled to Doctor Gregory's wrist. I crouch so that I am face-to-face with Wildgirl. 'We have to get out of here, right now.'

'Why don't we just talk to him?'

'The Elf steals my lighter and what does he do? He calls Doctor G, who comes as soon as he can. Don't you see it's strange?'

Wildgirl thinks it through. I don't want to keep whispering with the men nearby, but I have to convince her.

'We need to get out of here.'

'How?'

'Here's how it's going to work, children,' Doctor Gregory's voice rings out again. He sounds like he's wandered closer. 'You have something of mine; I have something of yours.'

Something of his?

'One of my employees, it seems, has been quite careless with company property. And one of you has been less than scrupulous in your dealings with it. You give me my bankcard, I'll give you your lighter, and we can forget the whole thing. I'll even overlook any charges made in the course of the evening.'

Shadows settle over Wildgirl's face. She's not going to give up the card without a fight. Doctor Gregory speaks again. The man does not shut up, ever. 'There's some very pretty engraving on this lighter. What is it? A "G" and an "O". What can that mean?'

I'm too busy looking at my shaking hands to stop Wild-girl when she steps into plain view.

'How do you want to do this?'

'No!' I whisper, but she moves out of sight.

'Let's be straightforward about this—you hand me my card and I hand you the lighter.'

'No.' Wildgirl tries to sound confident, but her voice wobbles. 'You put the lighter on that gallon drum over there, the blue one. And I'll put the card on top of those tins. And then we can retrieve our things. But I don't want you or anyone coming near me, right?'

Doctor Gregory laughs without warmth. I've got to get Wildgirl off the roof. This has nothing to do with her. I don't believe for a second that Doctor Gregory cares about the card.

'Very well, young lady. We'll play your funny little game, if it pleases you. Hold up the card now so I can see it for a second. I want to make sure it's mine.'

Wildgirl steps back while her hand is in the air, so she enters my line of sight again. Doctor Gregory's footsteps sound out, crisp and sharp. He must be putting the lighter down on the drum. It's almost impossible to make a clear plan when I can't see what's going on. Wildgirl doesn't look at me when I whisper. 'Is the Elf still there?'

'Nope.' She replies without moving her lips or turning her head.

'Put the card where you said you would. Then run for the door. I'll keep them busy.'

'The lighter?'

'I'll get it,' I say. 'Meet me in the tunnel.'

I stand up and watch through the rip in the sheet. When Wildgirl puts down the card I spring into action. I lift the ladder like a battering ram, and charge towards the nearest suit, screaming. Wildgirl sprints for the door.

Doctor Gregory lets her go without a second glance.

The man ducks as I try to clobber him with the end of the ladder, and then darts behind me. I swing around, hoping to collect him on the way, but he's too fast. He jumps on my back and clasps his hands against my throat. Something in my backpack presses against me painfully. I let the ladder fall and work on shaking him off. I growl and snap my head backwards, colliding with his nose. There's a squeal as the man slithers to the ground.

I've only got a few seconds to decide how to play this. I bring on the crazy-eyes and feign confusion, all the while checking out possible paths of escape. The man who attacked me has crawled away, leaving a trail of blood. I'm not sure I can outrun three of them.

'How are you feeling, Jethro?' Doctor Gregory cocks his head like a curious budgerigar. 'You haven't replied to any of my letters. I'm beginning to think you don't like me.'

I snarl, baring my teeth. I don't want them any closer. The guy I headbutted is on his feet again, by Doctor Gregory's side. The other bodyguard, taller and thinner, completes the trio.

'Did it feel good?' Doctor Gregory inquires. 'Hurting Delany like that?'

Delany glowers. The lower half of his face is sticky with blood and saliva and snot. A purple bruise is already spreading from his nose into his eye sockets. I had no idea I could do that with one blow.

'It must feel good to give way to your animal side,' continues the doctor. 'To obey your *true nature*.'

I remember the trowel on the side of my pack and bend my arm up to reach it. Doctor Gregory is watching my face so intently he doesn't notice the movement, but Delany is watching every little thing I do. The trowel comes loose in my hand and I lower my arm.

'I'm really interested in your situation, Jethro.'

Doctor Gregory takes a step forward, his hands steepled in front of his stomach like a priest or a politician. I flinch and jab the trowel at them. I back away towards the edge of the roof.

Doctor Gregory stops, and holds his hand up to keep his bodyguards at bay. I can't tell if he's trying to make me angry or placate me. He holds up the lighter.

'I want you to consider me your friend,' he says, and

throws it to me. I catch it with one hand and automatically put it in my pocket.

'You could come live at the institute. I know more about your condition than you realise. I'm happy to share what I know. There are others of your kind there. I think you would find that comforting. After all, you don't have anyone left, do you?'

Others of my kind. Maybe even a cure, or at least an explanation. He's bluffing, isn't he?

The tall bodyguard strokes something at the side of his leg. I stare at his hand until I figure out he has a pair of handcuffs hanging from his belt. They mean to take me with force. The doctor's smarmy voice rolls on.

'Your little girlfriend's abandoned you. No parents, no brother…'

I leap up onto the concrete barricade as swiftly as I can without losing my balance. The trowel drops to the ground and bounces away. I straighten my legs until I'm more or less upright. The parapet is about a foot wide. I keep my arms out for balance, and I avoid looking to my left, at the yawning twelve-floor drop.

If animal is what they want, then animal is what they'll get.

I face the men and growl, with my lips pulled back and my head shaking from side to side.

Doctor Gregory shouts a quick warning to his

bodyguards to hang back. All three men look up at me with expressions that are equal parts horror and fascination.

'Hold on, Jethro—' the doctor starts, but I'm away.

I run along the knife-edge of the parapet with the biggest strides I dare. I howl as I run, high and loud as I turn the first corner. I run faster up the next length towards the glow of the doorway. I leap back down, hitting the ground running and hurdle a stack of milk crates that blocks my path. I'm close to the door when—SLAM!

I run at full speed into the taller bodyguard. He barely stumbles and has time to land a punch in my gut. My vision dims. When it clears I slam my right fist into his chest. I follow up with my left, barely looking at my target. I feel the bodyguard's skull as my knuckles connect. I don't stop as he hits the ground.

I run towards the yellow glow of the only exit. I clock Delany trying to intercept me, and behind him the dark floating smudge of Doctor Gregory. Delany is too slow.

My feet act on their own, carrying me through the doorway and down towards the stairwell.

I look back to see Doctor Gregory standing in the doorframe. He watches me go, smoothing his hair with one hand.

I have the basement door open when I hear it. Reverberating around the stairwell.

A howl.

A long, strangled howl that could only come from Wolfboy.

The sound of him in pain.

I reverse back up the stairs without thinking, covering a flight before I hesitate. What if it's a trap? What if I make it worse? I'll be useless in a fight.

I turn around and keep going to the basement. Tears start falling and they don't stop. The metal grate still lies on the floor at the entrance to the tunnel. How long has it been since Wolfboy and I were here? I stare at the square opening. It doesn't look so appealing now that I'm on my own. I pick the grate up; I can balance it against the entrance to make it look as if it's sealed. I position myself to crawl into the gap, and pull the grate until it lies along the edge. I slide onto my stomach and push myself in backwards. I hope that I'll be able to hold on to the edge with one hand, and drag the grate with the other. But as soon as I slide past my ribs I fall all the way, losing my grip. My hands scrape against the tunnel wall. 'Shit!' I say, to no one in particular.

The tunnel is empty, but I don't feel like waiting underneath the entrance, exposed. I nurse my hands and walk until I spot an alcove in the wall behind a bundle of pipes. I bend down for a closer look. The space is bigger than I expected. Someone has turned it into a cubbyhole, with blankets and cushions.

My ukulele jams against the pipes, so I slip it off and crawl into the cubby. I sit on a cushion and wipe my face with the corner of a blanket. I am completely and utterly out of my depth.

I wish I'd hurt my hands worse because it's what I deserve. I should have gone back but now it's probably too late. Wolfboy could be lying on the roof, bleeding or unconscious. Doctor Gregory and those men could load him into their car and drive away. This is exactly what I was afraid would happen. I've got nothing left; my wallet, phone and keys are in Wolfboy's bag. What am I supposed to do? Walk home and pretend none of this happened? That I didn't meet him, that he never existed?

I'll wait for ten minutes, or what I guess ten minutes to be. I don't want to go back out there. I don't want this to be the way it ends.

My eyes aren't closed long before I hear someone landing in the tunnel. I'm too tired to consider fighting so I just sit and wait. A face appears under the pipes.

Wolfboy looks as bad as I feel, but relieved to see me.

'Hey,' I say, as he squeezes into the cubby. I raise two fingers in the peace sign. 'Magic Happens.'

Wolfboy crawls across the floor and falls into me, burying his face in my neck. I have to bite my lip so I won't cry again. And then, embarrassingly, I do.

I cry for way too long in a very hiccupy and undignified fashion before pulling away to look at Wolfboy. His hair is mussed up and he has a scrape on one cheek. The fight has gone from his eyes.

'I didn't get the card' is the first thing he says.

The card is the furthest thing from my mind. I can scarcely believe that he's here, alive. I heard him howl like someone was stabbing him through the heart with the trowel.

'I don't care about that. You're safe. Did you get your lighter?'

He nods.

'That's good.' It's reassuring that we didn't do this for nothing, but the lighter seems less important now. 'I'm so sorry. It was my fault we got trapped.'

'Don't be stupid. It's no one's fault.'

Wolfboy's hand is grimy with dust and blood. 'Are you hurt?'

He follows my gaze. 'It's not my blood.' His hand trembles under mine, and I realise he's as shaken up as I am.

I touch his cheek. 'Are you sure you're all right?'

'I'm fine.'

I wipe my tears away again. I must look like shit. My glamour days are definitely over. 'What happened?'

'Doctor Gregory...' Wolfboy struggles for words. 'There's something really wrong with that guy.'

'He's a total creep. How did you get away from them?'

'I didn't know what to do, so I leaped up on the wall. Ran around the edge howling like a madman.'

'You *what*?' I try to picture the wind grabbing at Wolfboy, the enormous space above and below.

'I ran around howling and they all watched me like I was a nature documentary.'

So that was the howling I heard. Some of the tightness in my chest dissipates.

'And then?'

'I made a break for the door. And then I took the stairs.'

'They let you go without a fight?'

Even as I'm asking I realise I already know the answer. Wolfboy's face flames with more than just the graze on his cheek. 'No. I took care of them.'

'Meaning?' I look at his bloody hand again.

'Meaning, I punched one of them in the head so hard I don't think he'll wake up until next year. And I head-butted the other one. Doctor Gregory watched me do it.'

Wolfboy's hands wrap around his head as if he's trying to hold the pieces of his skull together.

'I think I heard his nose break.'

'They were trying to hurt you,' I tell him, rubbing his leg. 'You had to.'

'It was like I was outside my body, watching myself do it. It was easy. But now I feel sick.'

'Because you're a good person. That's why. You didn't have a choice.'

He's still cloudy with doubt. Whenever there are fights at the Commons, the fighters always seem so proud after-wards, even if they've lost. It's never occurred to me that they might go home and feel ashamed.

'And you didn't see the Elf?' I ask.

When I came off the roof I was ready to do battle with my gardening fork, but the Elf was nowhere to be seen.

'No. I was so worried he would be waiting for you in the stairwell. When I saw the grate had been moved I knew you'd made it. And once I was in the tunnel I saw your ukulele.'

Wow. That was real smart of me. Maybe I could have flown some kind of welcome flag and let off a flare while I was at it. 'What do we do now?' I ask.

Right now the only thing I want to do is curl up and sleep for a few hours, but we're still under the evil empire, and not that well hidden. At least a few Kidds must know about these tunnels.

'I think we should see where the tunnel takes us.'

'Okaaay,' I say.

'I thought you were fine with being underground.'

'You didn't like it at first either. What if we're wandering around for days without food and water?'

'And in fifty years' time they'll find our skeletons, one of them with a bony hand extended in despair?' Wolfboy does a pretty hot impersonation of a grasping skeleton.

'Exactly. I could figure out the direction of the tunnels between the buildings in Orphanville, but once we go beyond that I have no idea.'

'We'll work it out. The tunnels will take us somewhere.'

I look into his eyes. I can only see their shine and not their colour in this light. I'm so glad he doesn't blame me. I don't know why I cried so much. It's not like me at all.

'And are you okay?' It's his turn to ask.

'I'm just relieved.'

Wolfboy looks a million times better than when I first met him. I know what lies underneath now. His patience. The way he'll make a joke and then look like he wants to take it back. How he listens to me, really listens. How he's survived the terrible things that have happened to him.

He stares back, and we really *see* each other. Wolfboy touches me on the tip of my nose with one finger, making me smile. I move closer, very slowly. His breath is hot and short against my cheek. I close my eyes at the last minute, and feel his lips against mine. Soft. I let my lips rest on his for a few seconds and then I pull away. He gently pulls me back in.

twenty-eight

The ceiling is still high enough to walk upright, but the tunnel has narrowed noticeably. The walls are lined with orange styrofoam in parts.

'Is there any chance the Elf knows we're using the tunnels?' Wildgirl asks.

'I don't think so.'

I suppose while we were on the roof he could have followed our trail here, but I don't think it's likely.

'Blake said he could climb.' Wildgirl is anxious. 'I keep imagining I'm going to look behind us and he'll be crawling on the ceiling like a spider.'

There's a comforting vision. I stop and face her. It's too easy to get spooked in the Darkness. You have to keep on top of your more paranoid thoughts. 'I think he went to find the rest of the Six-Sevens,' I say. 'He would have won big points with Doctor Gregory for luring us to Orphanville. That would have been enough. He won't bother us anymore.'

Tonight at least, I think, but don't say. We pulled the grate back over the entrance and secured it to some pipes with the rope I had in my bag. Of course there's the basement entrance in Seven and more in other buildings, but the acoustics are so good down here we'd get fair warning. There've been no obstacles so far and we've made good progress.

'Was that what this was all about? Luring us to Orphanville?'

I hold my arm over a low part of the ceiling while Wildgirl passes. She has something blue and spangly wrapped around her head like a turban. No one else could get away with it. She looks beautiful.

'I don't know what to think.'

Doctor Gregory had done his research. I was his mark, and he thought he knew how to get me.

'We walked right into their trap.'

'Yeah. They knew I wouldn't let the lighter go easily.' The problem was, I almost did let it go. If it wasn't for Wildgirl I might have. It turns out I'm more of a coward than they thought I was. 'Maybe they didn't expect me to do anything about it tonight, but—'

'Why didn't they just ask for the card? I would have handed it over. Why go to all that trouble?'

'I don't think the card has anything to do with it. The Kidds only saw you with it at Little Death—after they stole the lighter. They didn't know about it when they mugged us.'

'Then why?'

I sigh. Doctor Gregory knows too much about me. The way he stood there and fixed his hair, watching me leave. He didn't look worried about letting me go. He looked like a man who was biding his time.

'I think he wants to collect me, like a specimen in a jar,' I say eventually, even though I'm sure it's more complicated than that. Somehow Doctor Gregory got what he wanted, even though I got to leave with the lighter.

'If they didn't give a shit about the card I wish they could have let me keep it.'

'And have you run around spending their money? I don't think so.'

The tunnel broadens again and we follow it to the right. So far we haven't reached any intersections. That's when things will get tricky.

'Wait, Wolfie!' Wildgirl pauses and looks directly upwards. 'Did you see this?'

I join her. I missed the barred hole with fresh air

flowing through it. The night sky is visible. I brace my arms against the walls, and then step up on some pipes, so that I'm closer to the ceiling. I can't see anything more, but I can smell fresh air. It's quiet above ground.

'Do you think we can get the cover off?' Wildgirl asks. I run my fingers around the edges of the hole, and it feels like the bars are cemented in.

'No. It's good though because it means we're close to the surface. We should look for another exit close by.'

'Are we far enough away from Orphanville?'

'Yeah. I have a feeling we're near the memorial gardens.'

We keep moving forwards, passing a circular tunnel.

'What am I looking for?'

'I'm not sure,' I say. 'Another grate, or a ladder, or a manhole.'

I reverse a few steps and look down the tunnel. It's pitch-black and oozes damp air.

'Do you think there's something down here?'

I shrug. I have a hunch, that's all.

'Hey,' Wildgirl says, 'let me into your backpack. I've got a light on my keys that I totally forgot about.'

I turn my back to her and feel her fumbling with the zip of my pack. It's a lot lighter now.

'I'm glad you hung on to your bag. I would have had to kick your ass if you lost all my stuff.'

I probably wouldn't mind that, although if I were given

a choice, I'd opt for another kiss. It's the first time I've been so close to someone since I've changed. Kissing felt better than I remembered, but it also felt like it was something I had to be careful about. It never felt that way before.

Wildgirl's keyring throws off a surprisingly strong beam. She stalks into the old tunnel, sweeping the light back and forth. After a few minutes lingering in the one spot, she calls out. 'Wolfie, come look at this!'

Wildgirl illuminates the side of the tunnel, which gives way to a narrow room. At the back of the room is a rusty spiral staircase.

It's hard to see where the staircase leads, but it can't be far. Wildgirl holds her keyring up as high as she can, but the dark eats up all the light. The staircase is big enough for only one person at a time.

'What if it doesn't go anywhere?'

'Let's find out. I'll go first.' She takes my bag and soon I can see only her legs, leaving me to climb in darkness.

I reach out to get my bearings, and find the walls wrapping closely around the staircase, as if we're climbing a smoke stack. My arms and legs don't straighten fully, and the narrow steps are more like rungs on a ladder. The black is so complete I can't see my own hands.

I'm confused after a few metres. How can we be climbing so far when we're just below the surface?

'I've reached the end.' Wildgirl's voice is stifled.

'Can we get out?'

I hear Wildgirl fumble with my bag. 'You've got a spanner in here, right?'

'Why?'

'It's locked.'

There's a dull clang as Wildgirl bashes the spanner against the lock. She swears and puts more force into her blows. 'Got it!'

Her feet disappear. She laughs above me, but the sound fades weirdly, as if she's falling upwards.

First air, then moonlight floods the staircase. I see a square of starry sky above, then I half-fall, half-crawl out of the hole. The ground is further away than I think it's going to be, and I tumble over with my arms shielding my head. When I come to a rest Wildgirl is at my feet, laughing and pointing. I look behind me.

We're in the middle of an empty pond. Behind me is a fountain decorated with cherubs and a horse. I recognise the fountain as the one at the centre of the memorial gardens, but I don't remember ever seeing the small door set into its side, a metre or so above the ground.

When Wildgirl stops being amused at my expense, I let her climb onto my shoulders while I stand on the stone rim of the pond. Only a few of Orphanville's towers are visible above the trees, but it seems like every light is on. Our escapades haven't gone unnoticed.

I lower Wildgirl carefully. She's starting to shiver despite her jumper and jeans. Even my breath is misting in the air. It's late. The night is always coldest before dawn, even though the sun won't rise over the gardens.

'What *is* that thing on your head?'

She takes it off and shows me.

'It's a jacket. I found it in the cubbyhole and thought it was cool.'

She wraps it back around her head, tying the sleeves in a knot at the back. 'I'm rocking the disco nomad look,' she says. 'It's going to be big next season, just you wait and see.'

No wonder she got along so well with Ortolan.

'Where do we go now?' Wildgirl looks suddenly forlorn. I wonder if she's thinking about the lost card.

'You asked me earlier about where Paul and Thom live?'

'Yeah.'

'Their house is nearby. We can clean up there, and figure out what to do next.' I don't want to go back to my house yet. I don't know what I'll find there. If Blake will still be around. Or if someone else will be waiting for me.

We walk up one of the many paths that radiate from the fountain, my arm across her shoulder, hers around my waist. I steer us across the shrivelled Oak Lawn, which is more mud than lawn now. I wonder how long we were in Orphanville. It must be getting close to dawn in the City. The night isn't going to last forever, not for us. The best thing I can do for Wildgirl is to get her home safely, even though I wish she could stay. I can think of a million things to show her now, and I would have had the chance to if Doctor Gregory and the Kidds hadn't waylaid us. I want to ask her if she thinks we'll get to hang out again but I don't know how to.

'Hey.' Wildgirl stops. 'Look.'

It takes me a few seconds to see what she means. All around us, peppered all over the Oak Lawn, are furry brown blobs standing to attention.

Tarsier.

They watch us solemnly as we pass through their midst, but they don't move.

'I guess they found their new home,' Wildgirl says. 'I still wouldn't mind one as a pet.'

'What would you call it?'

'Maybe Snoopy. Or Gerald.'

After the lawn we cross the main avenue. On the other side is a stone cottage with white shutters and a chimney and a wooden door. I pound on the door with my fist, but there's no answer.

29

While the outside of Paul and Thom's place looks like a gingerbread house from a fairytale, the inside most definitely does not. The cottage is a disaster-zone. Someone has been sleeping on the couch, and another bed has been made from two chairs and a door. There's a laptop and printer on a sideboard, along with a whole bunch of other stuff: textas, badges, t-shirts. An old-fashioned writing desk is covered with takeaway containers and LPs. One set of curtains has been ripped almost off the rod, and the room smells strongly of boy.

'So much for security,' says Wolfboy, shutting the front door and switching on an overhead light that doesn't work.

He turns on a table lamp with a colourful glass shade instead.

'What kind of house is this?'

'It used to be a historical museum; you know—come see how the old-timers lived. But when the Darkness happened everyone forgot about it until Paul and Thom adopted it as their bachelor pad. Funny, huh?'

'Yeah.'

That explains the odd mix of antiques and boy arte-facts. I spot a pair of jocks stuffed in a milk jug. Gross.

'They're definitely not home.' Wolfboy taps out a quick message on his phone. 'At least we can clean up.'

'Is that your polite way of telling me I look like shit?'

'You look great,' he lies. 'But there's a basin around that corner if you need it.'

I cringe when I see my reflection in the mirror above the basin. My glamour turban doesn't hide my frizzy hair and I have panda eyes. The rest of my make-up has worn away. I take the jumper off and wear the sequined jacket over my Wildgirl shirt. The eyeliner dissolves with water. I consider using one of the toothbrushes balanced on the basin and then decide I must be temporarily insane. Toothpaste and a rinse will have to do. I test my breath by holding my hand in front of my mouth. Sweet cheeses. I'm glad Wolfboy ate the same kebab as me.

When I return to the main room Wolfboy is sitting in

a rocking chair, hoeing into a chocolate bar. The plastic bag full of herbs is in his lap and the room smells of pizza. Wolfboy's cheeks are all chipmunky with chocolate and caramel. He holds out his phone so I can read the screen:

i'm in LOVE

capital letter love

Wolfboy grins. 'What you have to understand is that Paul falls in love at least once a week. But he won't be coming home soon. He and Thom have gone to a party in the bush.'

I can't take my eyes off the bag in Wolfboy's lap. We've had chocolate all this time. How could I not know this? My stomach gurgles. 'Have you got any more of those?'

'Oh, sorry.' Wolfboy offers me the bag. He holds my gaze a second too long and then looks down. I wonder if he's feeling what I'm feeling, that we are alone in a house together. It's not like when we were at Wolfboy's. Thank god Paul and Thom are undomesticated. Imagine if there was a giant double bed in the middle of the room. Now that would be awkward.

I fish around in the bag until I find a bar, tear the wrapper off, and cram the chocolate in. My mouth floods with sweetness. Small flecks of oregano have invaded my mouthful but I don't care. So. Good.

Wolfboy gets up to use the basin.

'I just realised we left Blake's bike by the fence,' I say to his back. 'Yours too.'

His voice floats around the corner. 'I'll get the bikes another time. If someone's pinched them then I'll get Blake another. I never ride mine anyway.'

I cram another bar in and find Wolfboy's bag lying near the front door. I lay the borrowed jumper flat and put my things in the middle. Wallet, phone, keys, lip balm, the coaster I nabbed from Little Death. My phone is still off.

Shit.

My mum.

Without a doubt I'm out past curfew, by hours.

She'll have no idea where I am. I've stayed out before, but usually after we've had a fight, and never all night. I always let her know where I am: it's part of the deal we have. I bundle my things in the jumper, but keep my phone out.

I sit on the couch and wait for my phone to power up. Wolfboy wanders back into the room with *no shirt on*, drying under his arms with a handtowel. His chest isn't as hairy as I thought it would be. I had my face right up close to his, my lips on his lips, less than an hour ago. My phone beeps once.

Twice.

Three times.

Four.

'Your mum?' asks Wolfboy. I have four messages—two voicemails and two texts. Oh god. I can't listen to the voicemail, not now. I scroll down to the text messages.

Baby, let me know you're safe. That's all.

My mum is the only person I know who uses correct punctuation in a text message, and refuses to abbreviate a single word.

And the second: *PS. I'm not mad. Stay where you are, but let me know you're safe.*

I'm not mad. Why wouldn't she be mad? She should be. Unless…I wonder if someone's told her about what happened at school. I can't think of anyone who would. I'm the only person in the Commons who goes to Southside. There's no way she could find out. Unless a teacher…?

When I look up from my phone Wolfboy has put on a different shirt and is looking at me, concerned.

'Who was that?'

'My mum.'

He sits in front of me, on the packing case that Paul and Thom use for a table. 'Is she going to ground you for life?'

'No. She wants to know where I am. Well, she doesn't even want to know that. She just wants to know I'm safe.'

'You've got a pretty cool mum, then?'

'Yeah. No. I don't know.'

I reach forward and grab his arm, feeling the muscle move under his shirt and skin. If Mum knows what happened, she'll go in to bat for me at school and probably make things worse. If she believes that it's not me in the photo, that is. My throat closes up. 'I haven't come clean with you about everything.'

Wolfboy instantly looks worried.

'I'm in the shit at school. That's why I came out tonight, and that's why I was drinking like a fish. When I found the card I thought it was the answer to my problems: I could just run away.'

'Did you get suspended or something?'

'No, nothing like that.' If I tell him more will he start to see my faults too? I take a deep breath. Wolfboy's told me the worst things about his life. I can do this.

'It's just that everyone hates me at school.'

'Everyone? Every single person in the school?'

'Seems like it. I can't figure out what I did. I know I'm not the easiest person to be around sometimes, but still...'

'Did you get into a fight?'

'Not really, not a physical one. It might be easier if we did just slap each other and get it over with. It's mostly this one group of girls, but they have sway in my year level. The government should probably hire them for their expertise in psychological warfare.'

Wolfboy shakes his head. 'I haven't known you for very long, but one thing I do know is that you're a good person. I can't imagine why anyone would hate you. Look at the way you got along straightaway with Paul—he's the world's most awkward person—and how you charmed the pirates and that guy in the elevator. Who could hate you?'

I rest my head on Wolfboy's arm. His kindness puts me in danger of crying again. I can't tell him any more. Everything at home is still waiting for me. The thought makes me feel exhausted to my core. I've got to go back.

'Can we rest for a little while?'

'Sure. I'm not tired, but why don't you lie back and I'll wake you in a bit?'

Wolfboy ruffles my hair. He looks like he's going to lean in and kiss me on the cheek, but maybe I flinch or have a strange expression on my face because he stands up and moves away. He makes himself comfortable in the rocking chair again and picks up a comic.

I take off my boots and sink into the couch. I'll just close my eyes for a few minutes.

30

I don't know where I am at first. There's leather under my cheek, and a square shape right in front of my face, so I can't be in my bedroom. I try to sit up, but I feel like I've been hit by a truck. I lie back down until my foggy head clears.

It takes ages for my brain to wake up and tell me I'm in Paul and Thom's house. I must have fallen asleep on their couch. It's still dark so I can't have been asleep for long. I sit up with a spinning head. Instead of making me feel better the nap has annihilated me.

Wolfboy is asleep in the rocking chair with an open comic on his lap and his feet resting on the packing chest. One hand is clenched around something small, the lighter

I think, and he doesn't make the barest of sounds.

I stand up and pad quietly to the window.

The gardens are greeny-grey and dark. There's another dead lawn behind the cottage, dotted with empty flower-beds. A gazebo on the far side, and then a patchy line of trees. Shadows everywhere; the moon tucked somewhere behind the house. I realise I could have been asleep for a long time: the darkness doesn't mean anything. I didn't notice the time when I turned my phone on. Another fairytale feeling creeps over me. Maybe I'm like the Japanese fisherman who parties on the bottom of the ocean with the beautiful princess for three nights, only to return to the surface and discover sixty years have passed.

I drink some water at the basin and then find my phone wedged into the back of the couch. 5:27 a.m. No new messages.

I sit on the couch with my bundle of possessions in my lap and watch Wolfboy sleep.

He's a long way under. Only the rise and fall of his chest let me know he's not dead. I notice for the first time how thick his eyebrows are. This is the first chance I've had to think beyond this night. What happens next? Wolfboy might think I'm great now, but how long will that last? It won't take long for me to mess this up. I'm not so deluded that I think it's all someone else's fault I don't have any friends at school. Wolfboy doesn't know me at all.

As I watch him sleep, something slides inside me, a lens slips away and everything looks different. I don't know him either. Take away the last seven and a half hours and he's a stranger.

The cottage is small and there's not enough air.

I realise that I can't stay here. I have to leave. Better to quit while I'm ahead.

I find a Sharpie and a scrap of paper on the sideboard. Wolfboy doesn't stir. I sit on the couch and write him a letter before I change my mind. At first I struggle for words, but then I just write whatever comes into my head. When the paper is full I fold it in four and leave it on the packing chest.

I examine Wolfboy's sleeping face for the last time, searching for the part of me that wanted to hold his hand, touch his arm, his cheek, to know his mouth, but there's nothing. It's better this way.

I sling my ukulele around me and carry my boots in one hand. The door creaks loudly. I don't look back. I step quickly down the cottage path and onto the main avenue, clutching my bundle against my stomach. When I'm a safe distance away I stop and pull my boots on. The temperature outside takes my breath away all over again. I follow a new path past a basketball court and a playground. Gravel paths slice the gardens into triangles and squares. One square is full of trees lying on their sides like toppled drunks. There's a road beyond the playground. I wonder how far I'll have to walk before I can get a cab.

When I reach it the road is dark and unpromising. I follow the edge of the gardens, walking until I cross another path. It takes me back towards the centre until I'm standing at the fountain again.

I've lost all sense of direction: up and down, as well as north, south, east and west. I look around me, at the horse rearing above the pond, and the gravel under my feet, and I don't know what to see or feel. There is nowhere comfortable for me at this moment.

I sit on the edge of the pond and stare into the night. The trees are dark, silent giants. Dead but still standing, like stars extinguished thousands of years ago that still twinkle in our skies.

I was going to have to leave Shyness anyway. I test myself by trying to imagine Wolfboy taking the train across the city to Plexus in broad daylight. I try to imagine what he would look like sitting in our tiny apartment eating biscuits with Mum. No. Ridiculous.

I want to cry, but I've cried enough tonight. There are no answers in the still, black park. Are there monsters in these woods? Are there monsters out there in Shyness, or Plexus, or is it all in my head?

There's a gentle snicker to my left. I glance across and realise I'm sharing the pond with a tarsier. It sits on the rim, a metre away, and looks ahead, unblinking. I click my tongue to get its attention.

Instead of turning towards me the tarsier swivels its head away from me, and keeps on turning it *almost three hundred and sixty degrees*, until its eyes look directly into mine. It's one of the weirdest things I've ever seen, and unsettling as hell.

It's enough to make me stand up and walk back towards the cottage. Each time my foot strikes the ground I hear the words *not-afraid*, *not-afraid*.

31

The cottage door is locked. I keep turning the handle as if a miracle will happen, but nothing changes. We just walked in earlier so I can't understand why the door won't open now. Maybe Wolfboy did something to the catch.

I'll have to knock.

It takes several tries but eventually Wolfboy comes to the door. He is still sleepy enough to be confused about why I am on the doorstep and not the couch.

I push past him, speaking quickly. 'Sorry. I went outside to pee. I thought I'd left the door open, but when I came back it was locked.'

I put my stuff down on the packing case and pocket

the letter as smoothly as possible. Wolfboy doesn't seem to notice.

'I forgot to warn you there's no bathroom.'

'It's okay. I went in the bushes outside.' I sit on the couch, right back where I started. My voice and my movements feel unnatural. The best defence is a good offence. 'Where do Thom and Paul shower then?'

'My house. Or they don't. There's a public toilet on the other side of the fountain but it's a bit of a walk. Did you fall asleep too?' Wolfboy asks.

'Uh-huh. How long do you think we were out for?'

'No idea.' Wolfboy rubs his hair and sits next to me. I chance a proper look at him. He looks like himself again, just with sleepier eyes and messier hair. 'So, I've been doing some thinking.'

My stomach lurches. 'Yeah?'

'I've been wondering if my parents know Ortolan is back.'

The nervous feeling goes away. I thought he was going to say something else.

'They never ask you if you see her?'

'I only ever speak to my mum, and I haven't called her in months. We never talk about anything important anyway.'

'You never wondered about Diana, about her kid, I mean?'

'I was younger when I first found out she'd had a baby. I didn't ask any questions. I just didn't think about it. But now that I am thinking about it, there's something I want to do.'

'What's that?'

'I want to speak to Ortolan. Ask her a few things.'

'That's a good idea,' I tell him. He's quiet while he twists his shirt-tails in his hands. 'You mean right now, don't you?' I suppose they do things at all hours here.

'I want to go before I chicken out.' He pauses.

'Do you want me to come with you?' I ask.

'I think I should do this on my own.'

'Oh.' I feel a twinge of disappointment, even though it was me who was doing the walking out not so long ago.

'I thought I could walk with you part of the way and show you where to get a taxi. Then I can go on to Ortolan's house.'

That sounds good. That sounds like a scenario I can manage.

'You're brave,' I tell him.

He gives me a funny look. 'You broke into Orphanville as well, remember?'

'That's not what I meant.'

Wolfboy has to message Paul to get Ortolan's address.

'How come Paul keeps in touch with her?'

'Because he knows I don't.'

Wolfboy turns off the lamp, and leaves the chocolate bars for Paul and Thom. I rescue the pair of jocks from the milk jug and stretch them over the lampshade, just to mess with their heads.

Wolfboy turns to me at the door. 'What did it say in the note?'

'What note?' The lie is automatic. I don't want him knowing how close I came to leaving without saying goodbye properly. I'm not sure he'd forgive me for that.

'The bit of paper you picked up off the coffee table and hid in your pocket.'

'I don't know what you're talking about.' As always, once I've started a lie I can't stop it. I'm too ashamed to explain my reasoning from earlier. He'll think I'm completely neurotic.

He shrugs and walks out the door. I catch up quickly and link my arm through his.

We cut through the backstreets of Shyness, walking on unfamiliar roads. The moon has moved again to hide behind a blanket of clouds. Or the clouds have moved and the moon has stayed the same. Who knows how anything works here.

'So you'll get to see the morning in Panwood.' I tug on Wolfboy's arm. 'Are you excited?'

'It's been a while.'

'I'd lend you my sunnies, but I left them at your house.'

'You left quite a few things at my house.' There's a pause. 'So…when do I see you again to give them back?'

'I thought you could deposit my stuff with some Kidds, and then I would try to break in to their secret hiding place and steal it back, and then escape, all without being seen.'

'Nice plan.' He smiles but doesn't press me. I wish he would. I should have just said 'soon' instead of making a joke of his question.

The low shapes of the residential area give way to larger industrial buildings with high brick fences and barbed wire. Some of the bigger buildings even have watch-towers and spotlights. We turn left into another never-ending industrial street. It's a long walk to Panwood from the gardens. I sigh. All the adrenaline has left my body. I might float away any second now.

'Has it really been just one night?' I ask.

'Does it really matter?'

'It'll matter to my mum.'

'I'm sure it's only been one night. Do you recognise where we are?'

'No.'

'Little Death is a street over that way.'

That makes sense. The street we're on is lined with miner's cottages like the streets around the club.

'We've come almost full circle. Ortolan lives off Grey Street.'

I still don't get what he means.

'Come on. You'll see.' He drags me by the arm. I need dragging. I'd kill for a cup of tea. Hot, sugary, milky tea. The backs of my legs ache. The miner's cottages end at a wide thoroughfare of empty shops and dead lampposts.

'Is this Grey Street?' I ask.

'Almost.' Wolfboy is rushing now, taking loping steps so that I can barely keep up. We reach an intersection with four wide streets running in each direction. 'That's Grey Street. And look. The Diabetic.'

Across the road is the green pub I met Wolfboy in, all those hours ago. The neon sign is still on and there are lots of people milling around for this late on a Friday night. Or early on a Saturday morning. The pub looks different from how I remember it. I feel like I'm time travelling. I try to imagine myself walking through those doors, tipsy on cheap wine, desperate to forget. I had no idea what lay ahead. The sky above the pub is purple, not black.

'What's going on?'

'I don't know.'

There are three police cars parked outside and yellow tape over the entrance. A group of people sit in the gutter. A solitary Dreamer wanders in the middle of the crossroads like a drifting iceberg.

Wolfboy pulls me away. 'Whatever it is, it's bad news.'

I look over my shoulder as we leave. 'I hope Neil and Rosie are all right.'

'They would have left hours ago. They'll be fine.'

We stop a little way from the intersection, outside a costume hire place. I find myself dragging my feet more and more. All of a sudden I have too many things to say.

'This is where I leave you,' says Wolfboy, facing me.

'Okay.' I look down. I hate goodbyes. Nothing I say now is going to come close to describing how awful and amazing and crazy this night has been.

'This is O'Neira Street. It's Panwood from this point. If you walk up here for a few blocks you'll see a shop that sells exercise equipment, and some restaurants. There's usually a few taxis waiting there.'

'Got it,' I say, when really I took in only half of it. 'Which way are you going?'

'Back up Grey Street.'

Wolfboy hugs me tightly and I press my face into his shoulder. I try to record every little detail of the moment. The time comes when I have to pull away. I take the letter from my pocket. It says some of the things I want to say.

'This is for you. Read it later.'

'Is your phone number in here?' At least he doesn't tell me off for lying earlier. I fold his fingers over the letter, crushing it.

'Just keep it.'

Wolfboy bends down and kisses me, only for a second, but it's long enough. I keep my eyes on his, taking a mental picture, then I turn and walk away.

thirty-two

       The sound of Wildgirl picking tunelessly on her ukulele fades as she walks away from me. I wait until I can't see her sparkly jacket anymore, and then I turn onto Grey Street, only crossing over to the Panwood side once I'm well past the Diabetic.

There's not much happening on Grey. The only other people I see are inside a bakery, loading loaves of bread onto wide metal trays. I stop for a moment and check the directions Paul messaged me. I turn when I see the right street name and glimpse the first signs of dawn over the zigzag roofs.

My legs feel weak and I regret not bringing Wildgirl with me. Maybe I can't do this on my own. My fingers brush against paper when I put my hand in my pocket.

I sit against a fence and read her letter. Her writing is loopy and messy.

> *Dear Wolfie*
>
> *If it wasn't for you I don't think I would have ever discovered my true calling as a ukulele player, or the unpleasant knowledge that pirates are not the world's greatest kissers, or the pleasant knowledge that Wolfboys are.*
>
> *This has been some night.*
>
> *I'm hardly the right person to be dishing out advice, but if you were to ask me what I thought, I would say this: be friends with Ortolan. It would mean a lot to her and it wouldn't be bad for you either.*
>
> *Lecture over. Oh, STAY AWAY FROM KIDDS.*
>
> *Lecture over.*
>
> *This night was ours, just you and me.*

The letter is signed *NIA* xx, and there's a phone number scrawled at the bottom. I put it back safely in my pocket wrapped around my lighter. I feel ready now.

The sky grows lighter by the second. Streaks of nectarine-coloured cloud litter the horizon. I look behind me as I walk down the middle of the road, at Shyness, and all I see is bruised night. I wonder if Ortolan is the same as me, if she chose to live here so she could stay close to Gram.

I stop when I see the narrow two-storey shopfront.

The name, Birds In Winter, is spelt out in fairy lights in the front window. A corrugated-iron porch curves over the ground floor, and there's a window above, on the first floor. Ortolan and a little girl perch there with mugs and a blanket. Ortolan has already spotted me coming down the road. I realise I have no idea what I'm going to say to her.

I wave.

The little girl waves back impishly and then vanishes. Ortolan stands up as I cross to the footpath. The shop door is painted blood-red, with a sign in the shape of a dagger hanging above. There are excited footsteps behind the door. It clicks, and then swings inwards.

I look down at the little girl wearing sky-blue pyjamas dotted with fluffy white clouds. She has the same bobbed hairstyle as Ortolan, and a pair of very serious and very blue eyes. She smiles shyly, and opens the door wider.

'Good morning,' she says.

Acknowledgments

I'd firstly like to thank Mum and Dad for their unwavering support. Everything I am, I owe to them. Thanks to Carly and Jacqui, for being older, wiser and always interested in their little sister's strange antics.

Huge amounts of gratitude to everyone at Text, but especially to Michael Heyward for taking a punt on me, my lovely editor Alison Arnold, publicist Stephanie Stepan and rights guru Anne Beilby.

I'm very lucky to be surrounded by interested friends, work colleagues and family, all of whom have spurred me on for years with the simple question: How's the book going? Thanks particularly to Emah Fox, who always insisted I was a writer, even when I didn't believe it myself, and to Andrew McDonald for being my sounding board. Thanks to Carly, Amy Tsilemanis and Michelle Calligaro, who were very kind readers of my early drafts and, finally, thanks to my writers' week buddies, especially Jason Cotter for letting us invade his farm.